# TALES OF A SEA MONSTER

## LOU WILHAM

Midnight Tide
PUBLISHING

# Also by Lou Wilham

The Curse Collection
    The Curse of The Black Cat
    The Curse of Ash and Blood
    The Curse of Flour and Feeling

The Sea Witch Trilogy
    Tales of the Sea Witch
    Tales of the Littlest Mermaid

The Clockwork Chronicles
    The Girl in the Clockwork Tower
    The Unicorn and the Clockwork Quest

Villainous Heroics
    Villainous

The Heir To Moondust
    The Prince of Starlight
    The Prince of Daybreak

*For Lissa & Val,*
*who gave me the courage to*
*build worlds from words.*

# Tales of a Sea Monster

## AN ORIGINAL TALE OF THE SEA

## LOU WILHAM

## Prologue

*W*hat is in a name that makes a person who they are?

Is it memories, far more than a name, that make up a person? And what becomes of someone who has sacrificed those memories?

This is the story of how the Witch of the Deep found a new name, new memories, and a new life. Of how soulmates can find one another through great distances, and even time itself. Of how even without a past, there is always a future.

This is a story of hope.

## Chapter One

*N*ot remembering who I am should hurt more than it *does*, the beast thought. Not knowing her own name or if she ever even had one should scorch down to her very soul. But it never had. Or at least . . . not that she remembered.

All she remembered was the dark and the depths and the silence. The blessed silence that left her alone with the emptiness that was her own mind. *Which*, she reflected, *perhaps should bother me.* Perhaps the silence should have rung with the potential of unremembered things, an unlived life, but it did not. All it did was lull her into another deep sleep. Maybe this time when she woke, she would remember something of what she dreamed, instead of just the vague impressions of the Before. Or maybe she wouldn't wake up at all. *That would be preferable*, the beast thought, *easier*.

It was not so.

When she woke next, black eyes wrenched open, it was without memories as it had been for many a day—years, maybe. She had lost all sense of time down there in the depths. The Before lingered like the last rays of the sun on the horizon, just at the edge, and so *so* out of reach. Hard to look at and lacking the warmth of full day.

And there was no silence. There was the loudness of life. Grinding. Growling. Grumbling. Something raced through the water up above, large enough to dwarf the beast, but smaller than some of the other ships she'd sunk. Disturbed the peace that was the beast's home.

*How dare they. Foolish mortals.*

Didn't they know who it was they were disturbing? Had she not made it *clear* that they were not meant to travel her waters? The beast pushed off the wreckage of another ship that had dared trespass on her sanctuary and used her black flipper to propel herself toward the surface. As she went, she called upon the powers of the depths. The sea roiling around her, gaining life and anger of its own.

She broke the surface just as a dark cloud blotted out the once-bright sky. The crew shouted, trying to regain control of their little boat. Rain came down in sheets that made seeing which way they were going impossible.

Such a little boat in the middle of such a great big ocean. What hubris was this to think the sea would not swallow them whole?

Someone screamed, the sound shrill and manic enough to not be swallowed by the crash of thunder overhead and waves below.

"I see you, Witch of the Deep!" the voice cried. And when the beast's eyes looked up to find the person on the deck, she was pointing her way, finger shaking. The woman's hair was long and dark like the depths. It clung to her neck and waist, dragged down with rainwater. "I see you!"

*And I see you, land witch*, the beast thought with no small amount of disgust, but she did not shout back. There were faint flickers, traces of the woman's power clinging to her skin like wet sand. It didn't shine as brightly as a sea creature's might, but it was there just the same. The signal of another magic user in the beast's midst. Clearly, they had thought that bringing a land witch on their journey would protect them as they trespassed on the beast's solitude.

Clearly, they had been wrong.

Distracted as she was by the land witch's pointing and raving, the beast did not see the man off to her side raising a gun. She did not see him steady his arm against the rocking of the boat and take aim. She did not realize her mistake until it was far too late, and she felt the sting of the bullet lodge into her shoulder. It drew from her pale gray flesh a well of blood that looked black in the darkness of the storm.

*It does not hurt as much as it ought to*, she thought distantly. Likely because it was not the first time one of these foolish mortals had shot her and would not be the last. Her body was littered with scars—rounded, puckered markings where bullets had lodged themselves to be dug out by clawed fingers. But still it was enough to rile her to annoyance.

A writhing black tentacle of magic shot from the water and wrapped itself around the shooter's throat. He choked, dropping the weapon, and she tightened her hold until he was scrambling against the power, trying to pry it from himself. But how can one pry something from themselves that does not truly exist on the physical plane? They cannot.

The land witch screamed, spinning to try to help him free. But there was no use, for a moment later the beast had tightened her hold so much that she had snapped his neck. She felt the bones give way under her magic with a satisfying crunch, and then she let him drop down into the water below, eaten up by the turbulent sea. He'd sink to the depths, and there, the creatures—her creatures—would feast upon his flesh.

The beast was not sure why—perhaps it had been her thirst for blood sated, or the screams of the woman that had gone from manic to anguished—but she released her hold on the storm. She let the waves calm to a gentle rocking that the boat's puttering engines would have no trouble passing through. The land witch was still screaming, her fingers digging into the metal rail of the ship, looking as if perhaps she'd follow the shooter into the sea.

*Foolish. To give oneself over that wholly to another.*

The captain shouted, getting his crew moving again so that they could escape the water they had trespassed upon, one man short, but mostly unharmed, far more than any other ship that had trespassed in the beast's waters could boast. Another crew member came to drag the land witch from the railing as the beast watched. His arms wrapped tight around her as he said something the beast could not hear from where she floated in the slowly dying waves.

"You will pay for this!" the land witch shouted, her fingers white-knuckled around the rail, in spite of the man trying to pull her away. She was clinging with surprising strength. The beast could not see her eyes well enough, but she was sure the land witch was staring at her with a fury unlike the beast had seen from these mortals before. Or . . . Well . . . that she remembered, anyhow.

"I will see to it that you pay for this, Witch of the Deep!" The land witch spat the words as if they were a curse. "With your *life*!"

*I look forward to it*, the beast thought but did not say as she bowed her head to the land witch and sank beneath the waves. Back into the depths of her home. Back to the silence and the peace.

Still, something burned at her. And it was not the bullet

lodged in her shoulder that she would have to pry out before her skin could close back over it. No, it was something else. Something like recognition. Something like understanding.

She did not have memories of the Before. But now she was sure that in the Before she had loved someone that way. And they had been ripped away from her very similarly. Maybe that was what she had given her memories for . . .

Perhaps it was better to not remember the Before after all . . .

## Chapter Two

*A*lora remembered the stories of magic told by her great-grandmother Roan—Grandma Roan, for simplicity's sake. And how, as they grew up, fewer and fewer of her cousins would kneel at the little altar on the beach that Grandpa Jiro had built all those years ago for Grandma Roan. The one to the goddess of the sea.

Alora remembered the day the last of them stopped believing in Grandma Roan's magic altogether. The day the last of them knelt before the altar and prayed to Amphitrite. But Alora . . . Well, she never stopped.

And that was the crux of it. Alora had never stopped believing in magic. She had never stopped chasing it, either. She'd seen enough of it over the years to know just how real it was, and to know the rush of excitement that followed every new discovery. Like a buzzing under her skin. But seeing was not believing, at least not for everyone. And certainly not for Alora's mother, Cianna, who had raised Alora to be a logical, reasonable sort. Her words, not Alora's.

"You have a PhD in anthropology," Cianna said for

perhaps the tenth time that month, her voice tinny coming through the speakerphone and echoing off the stainless-steel counters. Alora had left her phone on the island so she could listen to music while she cooked, not receive yet another lecture on her life choices and how ridiculous she was chasing all those old fairy tales Grandma Roan had filled her head with. "I don't know why you don't do something useful with it."

"I am doing something useful." The words sounded trite even to her own ears. Likely because Alora had said them so much recently. Really, one would think an approaching birthday would be cause to celebrate, but not for Alora. Not for the family monster hunter. The black sheep. The weirdo. The one who refused to grow up, no matter how much Cianna pushed her.

"Chasing Bigfoot isn't useful."

"Hey." Alora pointed her wooden spoon at the phone, even though her mother couldn't see it. "Bigfoot is a myth. I proved that two years ago."

Cianna sighed, and Alora could hear the eye roll in the tone. It made her frown, her shoulders sagging. "Look. All I'm saying is you're almost thirty. Isn't it about time you settled down and did something—I don't know—*normal* for a change? There's a teaching position open at your brother's school. You could settle in one place. Have some grandkids maybe? You know. Leave the monster hunting to . . . less sensible people. Plus, it has to pay more than your little . . . show."

Alora bit her tongue to silence a reply and felt herself hunch a little more over the sizzling pan. What she didn't say was that it wasn't about the money or the fame or doing something everyone would recognize and appreciate or even believe. What she didn't say was that it was about the people she helped. The villagers and townspeople who had come to understand instead of fear their local boogeyman, or learned they didn't have one at all. Cianna wouldn't understand all that, because Cianna didn't believe such things existed. So, what Alora said instead was, "Sorry, Mom, I've got another call coming in. Love you! Bye!"

And then she hung up with only a twinge of guilt because it was only technically a lie. She *did* have a text notification from her teammate, Emrys, that said, "call me!!!!!!"

The line rang enough times that Alora half wondered if Emrys wouldn't pick up at all. When he did, she could hear wind in the background, and harsh pants like he'd been running.

"I'm booking you a flight," he said before she could even open her mouth to greet him.

"Hello to you too, Emrys." Alora snorted, turning back to the now mostly finished stir fry on the stove. "A flight to where?"

"Dent."

The wooden spoon banged too hard against the side of the wok. "I'm sorry. Did you just say Dent?"

"Yeah. You leave in . . ." Emrys paused for a moment, and Alora imagined him pulling his phone away from his face so he could check the time. "Five hours. Soooooo. You better get packing."

"That's ten at night." Alora huffed, turning down the heat on the stove so she could focus more on Emrys. "What's so important that I need to take a red-eye out to the country on a Wednesday?"

Emrys muttered something under his breath, probably hoping Alora wouldn't hear him. He did that a lot when he thought she was going to yell at him. Which was pretty regularly.

"I'm sorry? What did you say? It sounded like something-something ghost witch." Alora turned to the phone on the island, her hands resting on her hips.

"It just appeared, overnight, a few weeks ago." Emrys cleared his throat, maybe trying to play off the muttering from before. "They said it's flooding the town. If someone doesn't do something, they're going to have to abandon it entirely."

Alora sighed, blowing a strand of bright-red hair away from her face. "Is there any local lore about this thing?"

"None. It just sprang up out of nowhere. I've got the twins working on the research. Declan is already packing for us. We'll meet you at the airport at nine?"

"Eight thirty," Alora said, already spooning her food into a bowl so she could focus on getting everything she'd need together. "When will the twins be on the ground?"

"How did you know they were already on their way there?"

"Emrys."

"They should be landing within the hour. They've set up a meeting with the local historian. They said they'd leave the interviews of the townspeople to us." Emrys let out that uncomfortable laugh he always used when he was deeply dreading talking to people.

"All right. I'll see you there." Alora hung up, grabbed a fork, and went to stuff some fresh clothes into her go-bag.

THE TWINS, Bimala and Basanti, were waiting for them with a rental car out front when Emrys, Declan, and Alora got off the plane. Bimala was in the driver's seat, her long, neatly shaped nails drumming on the steering wheel, dark hair pinned back into a tight bun. Her twin in looks but not style sat beside her, fingers flying over a keyboard in her lap. Basanti didn't even have to be asked before she passed over a tablet loaded with everything they had found so far at the town records, and they were on their way.

"How long do you think it'll take us to hire a boat?" Alora asked, her eyes flicking over their findings quickly.

There was nothing about the lake the town was built near to suggest the kind of activity they were currently having. No past sightings. No legends. Nothing. Just the sudden appearance of some entity intent on drowning the town.

"Not as long as you'd think," Bimala said, her brown hand lifting to brush stray bits of hair back from where they'd fallen in front of her glasses. "The townspeople are pretty desperate. We were able to get someone to agree to take us out as soon as you came in."

"Were there any recent local deaths?" Declan peered over Alora's shoulder, trying to read along with her, his narrow chin digging into her shoulder.

"None on record." Basanti shook her head. There was a clacking from the front seat, and the brightness of her laptop screen was enough to burn Alora's eyes, but she didn't complain. There wasn't much time, not with how quickly the activity was increasing. A day, maybe a week, and everything would be under water. "But it looks like one of the locals just got back from some kind of trip around the world? She's got pictures of it all over her social."

"You think she brought something back with her?" Emrys leaned forward so he could peer at the screen from his seat behind Bimala, his blond hair almost blue in the dark of the car.

"Could be." Basanti hummed.

"Do you think you can handle checking on her on your own, Basanti? I'd like to have everyone else out with me on the water." Alora switched off the tablet, stuffing it into her bag. "If she's not in, you can head back to the hotel and start on b-roll."

"Yeah, I think I can do that. Looks like we should be arriving in town proper in say . . . an hour?"

"Midnight?" Declan gulped loudly beside Alora.

"Yes, Declan, that is what time it will be," Basanti said, and Alora didn't have to see her to know she was rolling her big brown eyes.

"The witching hour." Bimala cackled.

"I hate all of you." Declan huffed, blowing a long strand of black hair out of his pale face and sitting back in the middle seat with his arms crossed over his chest.

"You'll be okay, baby." Emrys patted his thigh.

"I AM NOT OKAY," Declan said, the fingers of his camera-free hand digging into the bright-orange life vest the captain had given him when Declan had expressed a fear of drowning. "How come Basanti got to stay on land?"

"Because she's running b-roll." Emrys wrapped an arm tightly around his husband's waist, trying to give him all the comfort he could.

"I could have done that."

"We needed you here to run the camera. Stop complaining, we're almost there." Bimala had moved to the bow of the little fishing boat, her knees pressing into the cream cushion that seemed to gleam in the moonlight.

"Yeah, that's what I'm afraid of," Declan muttered, likely thinking no one would hear him over the roar of the motor.

"What're we looking for exactly?" Emrys squinted through the haze of the gathering fog as if he couldn't make anything out. But Alora could see it in the distance. A tiny island with a tiny cabin on it. Glowing, almost calling to her.

"That." Alora pointed.

Then, it was like the fog cleared, and on the island stood a woman in a long white dress, her face turned up to the moon.

Something grabbed Alora—a cold hand with sharp nails, smaller than a man's, wrapped painfully tight around her forearm. Before she had a chance to gasp at the shock of cold, it dragged her over the rail, and she lost track of everything. Herself. The water. The boat. Time. Nothing made sense, and she wasn't sure which way was the surface anymore. Until the hand returned and grabbed her by the hair, then hauled her from the water onto the land.

There, she lay at a ghost woman's feet, no sound of a boat in the distance, only the pointed pounding of her heartbeat in her ears. The woman's feet were bare and pressed into the white sand of the beach.

"Aislin of Tjena," the woman said, her voice seeming to appear in Alora's mind as her lips didn't move.

"Alora," Alora corrected, coughing water from her lungs. Grandma Roan would probably tell her not to correct a ghost, but Alora wasn't exactly thinking clearly at the moment.

"Aislin of Tjena," the woman repeated, seeming not to have heard Alora at all. "You will bring me the heart of the Witch of the Deep."

"What?" Alora wheezed.

"You will bring me the heart of the Witch of the Deep, or I will take yours." The woman grabbed Alora by her collar and dragged her to her feet. Then, she thrust her hand into Alora's chest, meeting no resistance of bone or skin at all. Alora wasn't sure how, but she could feel the woman's cold fingertips brushing against the beating muscle of her heart. They closed around it, giving it one tight, painful squeeze that had Alora gasping. "You have until the blood moon rises."

The woman in white let go of Alora's heart, pulling her hand from her chest, and dropped her back into the water.

What felt like seconds later, hands grabbed at Alora's wrists and pulled her back aboard the boat. Emrys and Declan were looking at her with wide worried eyes. Bimala had gone very pale.

"Get her a blanket," Declan said, lowering her carefully to one of the cushions.

"Are you all right?" Emrys asked, fussing over her.

"Did you see her?" Alora coughed out more water, ignoring the way it collected in a puddle on her lap. "Did you see the woman in white?"

"What woman in white?" Bimala leaned in to wrap a blanket tightly around Alora's shoulders.

"On the island."

"What island?" Declan frowned.

"She pulled me over."

"No. We hit a wave, and you went over. Emrys and Declan got you back up right away." Bimala frowned. "Let's get back, you should get out of those wet clothes."

"Yeah . . . I should." Alora curled the blanket tighter around herself, ignoring the sinking feeling in her stomach that something wasn't right. She only looked around once, but when she did, there was no island. No woman in white. Just the fog, and the water, and the chill lingering in the air.

WHEN ALORA finally got them to stop fussing over her and leave her alone in her hotel room hours later, she tugged off her now-stretched-out, still-damp sweater and found five marks on the skin over her heart. Lifting a hand to the mirror, she pressed her fingers to the cool glass, lining each fingertip up with a mark.

Alora's heart gave a traitorously hard thump in her chest.

# Chapter Three

"*A*nd that wasn't there before?" Emrys asked doubtfully. He'd asked the same question at least five times after Alora had shown her team the mark left by the woman in white. Like he didn't quite believe what he thought was a figment of Alora's imagination could have left a mark on her. Sometimes Alora hated their resident skeptic. "It's not like a birthmark or something?"

"No. It wasn't. And no, it isn't."

"Are you sure?"

"Emrys." Alora eyed him with a frown.

"Just checking!" He held up his hands in surrender, taking a step out of swinging range lest she try to swat him.

"Women in white don't usually do things like that," Bimala said, her fake nails tapping loudly against her keyboard in the *clack clack clack* of near-panicked research. She'd looked up everything she could find on women in white from reputable sources and was now searching the unreputable ones. Looking for any kind of clue or answer. "They don't even usually talk. Just wail and cause a ruckus. Sometimes lead people off bridges, but . . ."

Basanti gripped her sister's shoulder tightly, and Bimala lifted one hand to pat at it. A silent communication between the twins that Alora had become used to. "What were her words exactly?"

"Well first she called me Aislin of Tjena, which is obviously not my name." Alora tapped her finger as if she were ticking things off a list. She focused on a spot on the wall behind Declan's head. "Then she told me I would bring her the Witch of the Deep's heart, or she would take mine. And then she said I had till the blood moon rises."

"I've done cross searches of the names Aislin and Tjena and not found them in any lore from around the world." Bimala pushed her glasses up her nose. "But you said you recognized the name?"

"Yeah . . . something in a story my great-grandma used to tell us when I was little." Alora huffed, flopping back into her chair and scratching at the mark on her chest. It didn't itch. It didn't hurt. But the knowledge that it was there when it shouldn't be crawled like bugs under her skin. Like when you touched something gross and had to wash your hands extra hard to get the feeling off of them. "I wonder if Mom would remember . . . or maybe Felipe . . ."

"No, you said they stopped listening to your Grandma Roan years before she died. You're more likely to remember than they are." Emrys shook his head. Declan had reached down to take his hand at some point.

Alora suddenly wished she had that—someone to comfort her in a moment like this. She didn't have a sibling who understood her, or a spouse who loved her, she just had . . . herself, and the monsters she chased in search of her next hit of adrenaline from grazing her fingers in the deep pool of magic. Taking a breath, she forced her mind away from those things.

"I *was*, but she died when I was ten. Do you know how

many things I remember from before I was ten?" Alora's fingers fisted in the blanket Basanti had laid over her legs. It was sweet, but unnecessary. If anything, Alora felt too warm. Like the room was stifling. She'd turned up the air conditioner the night before and still had to sleep without blankets.

"Just try?" Declan's tone had gone soft, encouraging. The way it went sometimes when he spoke to people in interviews. And she felt herself relax under his gentle coaxing, her mind casting back, just like his interviewees always did. He was so damn good at that: making people comfortable, getting them to talk, and being *sensitive*.

"The name was my great-great-grandmother's, Grandma Roan's mother's." Alora had kept that much of the memory intact, even if the rest of it had become fuzzy. She squeezed her eyes shut, pinching the bridge of her nose to ward off an oncoming headache. "Aislin died in childbirth, Grandma Roan said. She said her husband was forcing her to take potions to try to have a boy, but it had just been Roan and her six sisters."

"So that's something. The ghost thought you were your great-great-grandmother?" Basanti was trying to be empathetic, but she sounded doubtful. And she had a reason to be—this line of thought would probably go nowhere. Aislin was just an old fairy story Grandma Roan had made up to combat the loneliness of being an orphan; that's what Cianna had always said. "Tjena though . . ."

"It's where they were *from*." Alora lifted her head suddenly, her eyes wide. "Grandma Roan always said that before she'd met Grandpa Jiro, she was a mermaid. And her mother was from a village under the sea known as Tjena. That she was . . . That Aislin had moved from Tjena to become a seamstress." The words spilled out of her in a torrent, Alora's face lighting up with the memories of

Grandma Roan. They were still hazy, fuzzy around the edges, but they were slowly coming back. The more she said, the more she remembered. "And she'd had a best friend . . . no . . . a soulmate. A woman she loved. A sea witch."

Alora had always thought that part was romantic. The idea of soulmates and having one person who was meant for you in all ways. In spite of Aislin's end, Alora had always been a little jealous of Grandma Roan's mother for having that.

Bimala's fingers clacked against the keys, taking notes on everything that came from Alora's mouth with well-practiced ease.

"Mermaids? Like . . . *The Little Mermaid* kind of mermaid? Or like the scary kind?" Emrys asked, his nose wrinkling. They hadn't actually dealt with mermaids yet, and there were some things even Alora didn't think existed, but it wouldn't be the first time she'd been proven wrong.

"Sorta? I think? She never described the mermaids." Alora frowned. "When Aislin died, the witch vowed revenge on my great-great-grandfather, and there was a war. Grandma Roan said it went on for eighteen years. Until she went to the sea witch and asked for legs so she could learn about humans. That's how she met Grandpa Jiro."

"What happened to the sea witch?" Declan had scooted forward on his seat, his hands gripping the knees of his pants as he listened, enraptured by the story. It was rare any of the lore they found had romance in it, and Declan was a hopeless romantic, always looking for his next fix.

"I don't . . . I don't really know. Grandma Roan wasn't sure. She said the witch had to make a sacrifice to let her stay on land. I always kind of assumed she just . . . died?"

"Well, that's a terrible ending. So she gave up her life so

your great-grandma could be with the man she loved?" Basanti huffed, brushing her short dark hair out of her face so she could fix Alora with an unimpressed look.

"Grandma Roan never said what kind of sacrifice she had to make. Just that the magic it took to give her legs for the rest of her life had a . . . a cost. But that's just a story. Or that's what Mom said, anyway. She said Grandma Roan made it up because she was an orphan runaway and didn't want Grandpa Jiro looking for her parents."

"Then why did the woman in white think *you* were Aislin of Tjena?" Emrys tucked his hands into his pockets, looking distinctly uncomfortable with the talk of mermaids. He didn't get as squeamish about the monsters as Declan, but he wasn't a fanatic like Basanti tended to be.

"Grandma Roan said her people believed in reincarnation. That anything born of the sea would die and be reborn. The woman in white must think I'm the reincarnation of my great-great-grandmother. It's probably the hair." Alora pulled a long lock of red hair from her ponytail over her shoulder to look at it. "No one else in the family had red hair, and Grandma Roan said she'd gotten it from her mother."

"Well," Bimala said, shutting her laptop. "If this woman in white is connected to you via your lineage, and this story, I think the best place to start is your Grandma Roan's house."

"Why?" Declan turned to look at her. But Emrys had already pulled out his phone and begun to book them a flight.

"Basanti said Miss Archwood wasn't home. It looks like she dropped her luggage at the door and disappeared." Bimala bent to put her laptop back in the messenger bag at her side. "And since she's the only one who's been out of town recently, she was our only lead."

"There were sandy footprints on the rug," Basanti added helpfully, pulling up pictures on her phone. She held it out to Alora. "This is what she looks like."

Alora's brows pinched together, her heart giving a traitorous thud in her chest. "She looks a lot like the woman on the beach. I mean . . . I can't be positive, but—"

"Right. So she might be our girl. And even if she's not, her travels took her . . ." Bimala tapped on her own phone for a moment or two before she turned it to show Declan what she was looking at. Probably flight recorders, or some kind of itinerary, or maybe even just the woman's social media. Alora never knew quite how Bimala got her information, and she'd long ago realized it was likely better not to ask.

"Right in the neighborhood of Grandma Roan's house," Alora said without having to see whatever was on the phone. It was just the next leap in a series of leaps that didn't make a whole lot of sense, but also made complete sense. Eliminate the impossible, and whatever remains, however improbable, must be true. It was Alora's mantra, her way of seeing the world, the only thing that made sense sometimes when faced with magic and boogeymen.

"I hate when magic things line up like that." Emrys sighed loudly, flopping into Declan's lap. "Why can't they just be a single incident? Why do they always have to have some weird connection to another place? Or, like, a blood feud or something else stupid. What's with magical creatures and blood feuds anyway?" Declan patted his head sympathetically.

"I'm going to look at maps of the waters surrounding your grandmother's house," Basanti volunteered, ignoring Emrys's complaints as she snatched Bimala's phone from her fingers. "It looks like Miss Archwood was out on a boat during her time there, according to her social media. Maybe they went over wherever this Witch of the Deep lives, and that was the catalyst."

"Do you think it's connected to the sea witch?" Declan looped his arms loosely around Emrys's waist, giving him a squeeze until he stopped his whining.

"It's been over a hundred years." Alora frowned, pulling her legs up onto the chair to cross them beneath her knees.

"How long do mermaids live?"

"I don't know . . . I guess they could live for centuries, if they're real." Alora frowned thoughtfully. "I guess we'll find out."

"Mermaids." Emrys laughed, thumping his head against Declan's chest. "Ghosts, I get. Demons, even to some extent, make sense. But mermaids?"

"This isn't the first supernatural entity we've encountered that didn't have human origins," Bimala said.

"Remember the gremlins?" Basanti peeked up from the phone, biting back a giggle.

"Ugh, the gremlins! I've just grown back my eyebrows." Emrys flopped more dramatically against Declan.

"Try not to think about it too hard, love," Declan murmured, rubbing soothing circles into Emrys's thick flannel.

"JUST PUT YOUR STUFF DOWN ANYWHERE," Alora said, setting her go-bag down on the cabinet by the door. The house smelled a little musty from having been closed up for so long. Alora would have to talk to the caretakers about opening the windows more when the weather was warm.

"Wow . . . all this is yours?" Declan rocked back on his heels with a whistle.

"Yeah, Grandma Roan left it to me when she passed.

But she set up some caretakers to look after the place until I was old enough." They knew that. She'd told all of them about the house on the sea that she'd been left in passing. But they'd never been there. Alora couldn't pinpoint the reason why, but there was something almost . . . uncomfortable about sharing this piece of herself and her home with anyone who knew her, even her team. Still, the cat—or the fish, rather—was out of the bag now.

"And why don't you live here?" Bimala moved into the living area to settle her laptop on the old coffee table.

"Because I like where I live." Alora shrugged. "Plus, it's just me. Seems a waste. I rent it out in the summer."

"Why not sell it?" Basanti moved to one of the crammed bookshelves along the wall, her eyes roving over the thick leather tomes Grandpa Jiro had left behind.

"I can't."

The group turned to blink at her in curiosity, but Alora didn't really feel up to explaining her attachment to the place, or the way the sea air settled into her skin like a blanket, so she headed through the open first floor to the doors at the back. "I'm going down to the beach for a little bit. Gotta check on the shrine. I had the caretakers put fresh linens down before we came. You guys should go up and take a nap or something. We've got a lot of work to do."

"I'll go down with you." Basanti dropped her bag next to the shoe rack. Alora opened her mouth to tell Basanti she didn't need to, but Basanti held up one brown hand and offered her a tilted smile. "A couple extra prayers to the goddess of the sea can't go amiss where we're going, can it?"

"I guess not." Alora sighed, pushing open the glass doors at the back of the house and stepping out into the crisp night breeze scented like the sea and saltwater. The door shut behind them with a faint click, and Alora sat on the steps to take off her shoes before treading into the soft, cold sand. It always felt softer at night, like the coolness of the air and the bath of moonlight made it velvety instead of coarse.

"You're not really going to cut the heart out of this Witch of the Deep, are you?" Basanti asked, her voice soft enough that it was almost lost in the comings and goings of the waves.

"No. I'm not." The little altar by the sea was tucked away beneath a rock face, protected from the weather. Someone had placed fresh flowers there recently—daisies lay before the little statue of Amphitrite.

"Then what do you plan to do?"

"I don't know yet. We've got to find the witch first."

"Alora, this isn't about—"

"This isn't about us, Basanti." Alora sighed, lowering herself to her knees. "Now be quiet. I have a goddess to speak to."

## Chapter Four

*I*t *hurt*, the beast noted with some small amount of annoyance, glaring at the still seeping bullet wound. She could not remember when it had happened, or how, but she knew that it seemed to be infected. That was the tricky thing about living underwater: open wounds needed to be tended properly or infection was inevitable. And this infection was spreading dark lines down the length of her gray-brown arm.

She poked at it with a clawed finger and hissed when it irritated the already inflamed skin. There was nothing for it; the bullet would have to be removed. The beast nodded to herself and shifted so she could get a better look.

*Still, it is quite pretty*, she thought idly, watching the dark crawl under her skin, like lace. Maybe she'd leave it and see how long it would take to kill her. Maybe she'd tally the days somewhere, actually put effort into knowing how many of them had passed. Something to look forward to.

She was jerked out of her musings by the sound of an engine overhead. She squinted against the bright sun, watching the bottom of the boat come into view.

*Stupid mortals, and their stupid boats. Have I taught them nothing?*

Using her fin to press off from the boards at the bottom of the sea, she propelled herself toward the surface, taking the rage and pain of the deep with her to form a thick miasma of dark tentacles that seemed to writhe and twist of their own accord. The storm swelled up around her, covering the sun in thick clouds.

"Does anybody see it?" someone called from the deck. The woman squinted into the already pouring rain, a pair of binoculars thumping hard against her chest.

"We don't even know what we're looking for!" A blond man's head swiveled, his shaggy hair falling into his eyes.

"You'll know it when you see it," an older man shouted from the helm, his hands white-knuckled around the wheel. "You kids just be careful! It'll pull you overboard before you can blink!"

The boat rocked, tipping the red-haired woman dangerously close to the rail.

"Alora! Get away from there! If you go over —" But the black-haired woman's words were swallowed by the crash of thunder overhead.

"I'll be fine, Basanti, chill out," the woman with the binoculars — Alora, it seemed her name was — hissed over her shoulder. "I think I see something."

*Stupid humans. Come to gawk at me.* The beast rolled her eyes. She'd give them something to gawk at. She rode the swell of a wave, letting the lightning make her clearer to the people on the ship.

Alora lifted her binoculars, and the beast could feel the moment Alora's gaze settled on her. Like something crawling under her skin that was no infection. Something warm. Alora gasped, her mouth falling open, and she lost her hold on the binoculars. The strap chose that moment to snap, and they tumbled down toward the riotous sea below. Alora's hands scrambled for them. She leaned forward over the rail. One giant wave rocked the boat, and she went over.

"Alora!" the rest of the passengers screamed over the sound of the storm.

"Somebody, get a rope!" another man shouted; his dark hair slicked into his eyes. "Alora! Can you hear us?"

"We've got to get going!" The man at the helm had kicked the motor into gear again, it was so loud. "You've seen the witch, and it's had its pound of flesh. We have to go before it gets hungry for more!" He was muttering something under his breath about warning them and signing waivers, but the beast didn't pay him much mind because none of those things made any sense to her.

What happened next, the beast had no explanation for. She could not make heads nor tails of why she dove into the depths after Alora. Maybe it was the words of the captain. Or maybe it was the delirium of the infection taking hold of her senses. But she found Alora in the murky depths, her red hair like a beacon in the night.

Alora wasn't struggling like most mortals did when they lost themselves to the sea. Her eyes were wide open, and she almost looked as if she might be breathing under the water as she let herself sink. Which was . . . impossible. Then she spun, and the light from the surface caught on the green of her eyes, and something in the beast screamed, *I know you!*

The beast did not question the notion; she pushed herself forward through the water, her fin flapping madly, grabbed Alora by the waist, and tugged her to the surface. Someone on the ship was fighting the captain for the helm, and two humans had lowered a rope into the water.

"Alora! Grab on! We've—" the blond man stopped, his eyes wide in his face as he stared down at the beast.

"Let her go!" a woman with short black hair screamed, her hands tight around the rope. "You let her go!"

"It's all right, Basanti," Alora said, her voice loud in the beast's ear, but even for as calm as Alora sounded, the beast could feel her heart pounding in her chest, her body tense and uncomfortable in the grip of a beast. "Just throw me the rope."

The man didn't have to be told twice. He tossed it to her, and Alora took hold. The beast waited until she was sure Alora was safe on the deck of the boat before letting herself sink back into the depths. Basanti was bundling Alora up in a strangely stiff blanket, the man hustling them away from the rail and out of the beast's sight.

So focused on catching every last glimpse of red hair, the beast didn't even see the captain throw the net. It smacked against her head, the weights beneath it drawing it around her flailing limbs.

The captain crowed.

The beast tugged, intending to pull the man into the water with her if she had to, if it was the only means of escape. But he had some kind of mechanism—the beast could hear it above the slowly dissipating storm. It was cranking and grinding, tugging her toward the surface even as she struggled toward the depths. She could use the magic, she knew that, but it was a danger to the other humans on the ship. To Alora. And so, the beast didn't call upon the depths to save her.

The net lifted her out of the water before she even fully understood what was happening. She swung above the deck, her eyes narrowed on the man as he rubbed his hands together in delight.

"And let it be said, it was I who caught the Witch of the Deep. I Captain Jack S—"

He was cut off by the connection of Alora's fist to his face. Captain Jack stumbled, holding his cheek and glaring at Alora.

"Cut her down, now. Or you'll be the one in the net, Captain Jack." Alora narrowed her eyes to slits, her jaw pressed so tightly that the beast wondered if her teeth were grinding.

"And do what? Put it back?"

"Yes! Put her back!" Alora growled. "She saved me; I'm returning the favor."

"Alora, think about this," Basanti said, reaching to take Alora's hand, but Alora jerked it away. "Remember the curse."

"Cut. Her. Down."

Captain Jack huffed, but he pushed a button on the panel beside him and the net dropped to the deck, taking the beast with it. The thump against the hard floor jolted the bullet wound, and the beast hissed, holding her injured arm tight to her chest.

"She's hurt." Alora blinked for a moment, then spun to the group that had assembled behind her. "Bimala, get the first aid kit. Declan, see to it that Captain Jack gets us turned back around to land. Emrys, come help me get the net off her."

The group didn't wait for further instructions. They sprang into action, and soon the beast was being crowded by Alora and the blond man, who must be Emrys. She hissed, using her tail to try to press herself away from them. Maybe if she could get herself back to the rail she could get over and back to the sea.

"Shhh. Shhh. It's all right. We're not going to hurt you. I promise." Alora held her hands out between them, hovering in the air, waiting for the beast to consent to her help. "We just need to see that wound, and then we'll send you back home. All right?"

The beast looked down at the lace of black veins under her skin. She would die. It would be slow. It would be painful. And she would die. But that was better, wasn't it? Alora didn't wait for an answer. She lowered her hand gently to the shining violet scales of the beast's tail to begin detangling her.

And that's when pain like the beast had never known before erupted from her tail, ripping a strangled gasp from her throat. Pale green magic burst to life from Alora's fingers. It spread from Alora's hand, outward, covering the beast's scales like a net. Cutting them away and stripping them down. Separating them and tearing through the beast until her vision whited out. She screamed, her throat raw with the sound.

Someone else was shouting too, the beast realized distantly. Alora, it sounded like. "I need towels!" and "Water!" and "Oh god, there's so much blood!"

THE BEAST LOST consciousness at some point, and when she opened her eyes again, Alora was there. They were in a room, and someone had moved her to a bed.

"You know," Alora said, a smile ticking up the corner of her full lips. There was a galaxy of freckles across her nose that seemed to smudge when she wrinkled it in amusement. "After all the stories we heard from the fishermen in the town, I kind of expected a bit more from you. Like some kind of giant squid or something. But you're just . . . Well, you're just a woman, aren't you?"

The beast narrowed her eyes. *Just a woman.*

"Not a fan of giant squids either, I take it?" Alora raised her red brows.

"Take me home," the beast croaked around her raw throat.

"Ah. She speaks." Alora sighed, the amusement slipping from her features to bleed into surprise and then some kind of resigned expression the beast didn't wholly understand. She pursed her lips for a moment then leaned back in her chair, which creaked under her weight. "I'm afraid I can't do that."

"You promised."

"I know I did." Alora nodded. "But I don't think . . . Well . . ." She pinched the bridge of her nose. "See for yourself."

Alora leaned in to pull the blanket down off of the beast's—legs! She had legs! Why did she have *legs*?

"What did you *do*?" the beast hissed, her talons clutching at the blanket so hard they tore holes in it. She reached for the magic within her, for the call of the sea, but it did not answer.

"I didn't do anything." Alora held up her hands in surrender. "All I did was try to get the net away from your tail, and this happened."

"You did some kind of magic! I saw it!"

"I don't know any magic." Alora frowned, a wrinkle forming between her brows. "I'm just a human. I can't even perform spells, and I've tried, trust me. They'd come in handy in my line of work. The best I can do is light some sage and cleanse a house. That's why I needed you."

"Needed me, *why*?" The beast tilted her head. She pulled the blanket back over her legs, not wanting to see the ghastly things any longer. They were making her sick.

Alora let a long breath out between her teeth that sounded almost like a whistle and tugged down the collar of her shirt to expose what looked like five bruises on her chest. Only . . . they seemed to be spreading, the discoloration bleeding out across Alora's pale skin. And in some places, it looked as if her skin had begun to flake away.

"This is a curse mark from a woman in white," Alora explained, fiddling with the collar of her shirt as if tempted to pull it back up so the beast could not see the mark the woman in white had left. "She said that I have until the blood moon to bring her the heart of the witch of the deep, or she'll take mine."

"So you intend to deliver me to her." The beast frowned at Alora. She did not want to live, but she did not intend to be a bargaining chip either.

"No. I went looking for you, hoping you could help me. I thought . . . Well, I thought that since you seem so powerful, maybe you could break the curse." Alora met the beast's eyes with an expression of earnestness. She meant what she said. How strange. "We've been looking for a month now, and I've finally found you."

"I cannot break or undo curses," the beast said, feeling only a little bad about it.

"Oh. Oh, of course." Alora nodded, her hand falling away from her collar where it hung oddly limp, the bruises of the curse mark still peeking out just over the top.

"Now can I go home?"

"Oh umm . . . sure. If we can figure out how to get your fins back. Yeah. I'll take you home."

"You do not know how to undo this?" The beast gestured to her covered tai—legs.

"No. But I'm sure we can find a way. It just might have to happen after we find some way to undo my curse. You can umm . . . you can stay here with Bimala while me and my crew work on the curse. She'll take good care of you."

The beast rolled her eyes, swallowing against a suddenly

dry throat. It had been so long since she'd had to speak to anyone. "I will come with you. Then we can search for both at the same time."

Alora seemed to perk up, her lips curling into another soft grin. "Really?"

The beast nodded, scratching idly at the bandage covering her bullet wound. She had a feeling she was going to regret this, but she did not see where she had much choice.

## Chapter Five

"*J* don't think it's a good idea," Basanti said, her arms crossed over her chest. She had one foot braced against the wall where she leaned outside of the bedroom they had put the witch in. Her dark fringe had dried and clung limp to her forehead. "We can't trust her. We don't even know what she *is*."

"It's a good thing you don't make those decisions then, isn't it?" Alora didn't stop to face Basanti. She let her steps lead her down the hall to the stairs. She was not in the mood to argue about this. They had work to do, and the clock was ticking.

"Alora." Basanti grabbed the back of her shirt, giving it a hard yank. "She's responsible for thousands of deaths in the last fifty years alone."

"And what would you suggest, Basanti? That we just hand her over to the woman in white?"

"She's killed people!"

"So had that forest spirit last year, but you insisted we give it a chance, didn't you?" Alora hissed, yanking her shirt from Basanti's hand. She bit down on the urge to call

35

Basanti out on the jealousy that colored her expression and stormed down the stairs. Bimala and Declan were pressed together on the couch, their heads ducked over a laptop screen. They didn't look up when she entered, but she could feel them watching her at the edge of their gazes.

"I made some soup for our guest," Emrys called from the kitchen as if he did not feel the tension in the air. Which was a bald-faced lie, and they all knew it. "It's vegetarian . . . all you had in your freezer was veggies and fish. And I didn't think she'd like fish . . ."

"What have you found?" Alora asked, ignoring him as she flopped into one of the armchairs that flanked the couch. She braced herself on her knees so she could see the screen before Bimala and Declan.

"Right. I'll just turn the heat down, so it stays warm." Emrys cleared his throat and went back to banging around in the kitchen.

"The shipwrecks in that area go back for a hundred years or so. Probably about the time your Grandma Roan says she got her legs." Bimala still hadn't looked up from the screen, and her tone was soft but professional. Alora was grateful Bimala had never picked sides when she and Basanti had broken up. She'd just shrugged it off and told them to deal with it themselves, like adults. And they had, for the most part.

"The records are spotty from the early 1900s," Declan picked up where she left off. "But there are none of Roan before she married Jiro. She didn't have any kind of identification, or family history. It looks like her husband had that all made up for her right before they were married. He claimed she was a runaway from some foreign country."

Alora snorted, rolling her eyes. "Of course, he did."

"So are we saying Alora is a mermaid?" Emrys asked, leaning over the back of the couch to hold a mug out to

Declan. Declan took it with a soft smile, pressing a kiss into Emrys's cheek.

"We're saying it's *possible* that Alora is *descended* from mermaids." Bimala tapped one perfectly manicured nail against the trackpad of the laptop, her teeth biting at the corner of her lower lip. "Which might explain how when you touched the Witch of the Deep, she got legs."

"Some kind of lingering magic in the bloodline," Declan mumbled into his mug.

"Very scientific hypothesis." Emrys huffed, wrapping his arms around Declan's shoulders to hug his back while Declan grumbled.

"You could try touching her again and see if she gets her tail back," Basanti said. Alora could see her out of the corner of her eye, leaning against the wall just at the bottom of the stairs, her shoulders hunched, her face ironed out to show none of her thoughts in its lines.

"I already did touch her again. Nothing happened." Alora leaned back in the chair, her head hanging over the backrest to stare up at the white-washed wood of the ceiling.

"But you didn't do it with intent."

"I didn't do it with intent the first time." It wasn't that Alora didn't want to send the Witch of the Deep back home. It wasn't. Because she most certainly did. She hated the way the witch looked so small in the bed upstairs. The lost look in those black eyes made Alora's heart clench painfully in her chest, more so than when the woman in white had grabbed it. It was just that she didn't know *how* to get her there.

"Well, you must have done something because—" Bisanti pushed off from the wall to make her way over to the little sitting area.

"Enough," Bimala said, her eyes narrowing on her

sister. "It'll be better if we take her with us. Then if we encounter the woman in white again, we can protect her."

"Protect her," Basanti scoffed.

"Basanti. I said enough."

"Fine. Whatever."

"Now that that's settled, where do we start?" Declan asked, jiggling his finger on the trackpad of the laptop to wake it back up.

"We should reach out to some of our contacts from other jobs." Emrys straightened up. He pulled his phone from his pocket to start scrolling.

"None of those were sea related." Declan wrinkled his nose.

"It doesn't matter. Any supernatural or magical help we can get is a good place to start." Emrys waved his hand as if brushing off the thought. "Bimala, see if you can find any locals we can talk to too. Palm readers, psychics, mediums, anything. Weed out the ones that look like frauds."

"Already started." Bimala grinned a little. "You're behind. As usual."

"Rude." Emrys clicked his tongue, but his eyes had crinkled a little in amusement.

"I'm going to dig around in Grandma Roan's room and see if I can find any journals or anything." Alora pushed off her knees to stand. "Declan and Basanti, can you two look through the books down here? I doubt she'd have left anything out in plain sight, but maybe Grandpa Jiro had some books on lore? I think he and Grandma Roan wrote a dissertation when they first got married about sea mythology. See if you can dig that up somewhere."

"There might be some lore about the shipwrecks too. It won't be correct, but it would be a start." Declan rose, stretching his arms so his elbows popped softly. Then he turned to Emrys to give him his biggest puppy dog eyes and held out the empty mug. "Coffee?"

"You'll never be able to sleep tonight if we—" Emrys sighed. "Fine. I'll put on a pot."

Alora shook her head fondly and headed back to the stairs, ignoring the feeling of Basanti's eyes pricking on the back of her neck. She heard Basanti mutter something about Alora letting that creature stay in her room right before she turned the corner on the landing. But she left it at that. They didn't have time for more fighting.

"WHAT ARE YOU LOOKING FOR?" the Witch of the Deep asked, her eyes narrowed in annoyance at Alora, who was digging through a trunk at the foot of the four-poster bed.

Alora had been trying to be quiet, she really had. She was sure the Witch of the Deep needed her rest, but after a half an hour of fruitless effort, she still hadn't found any writings from Grandma Roan, and her movements had become more frustrated.

"I asked you a question," the witch said in a tone that demanded an answer, the long, dark talons on the ends of her fingers clutching the blanket that she'd pulled up to her chin. It made her look like a scared little girl, Alora realized, swallowing around something fierce and protective in her chest.

"I'm looking to see if my grandmother left a journal or anything behind. It might help us get your tail back." Alora leaned back on her heels, running her fingers through her long red hair to try to ground herself, to steady the way her heart leapt a little at the witch's quiet, rough voice.

"Why would your grandmother know anything about my tail?" The witch sat up a little, her eyes widening as they fixed on Alora, and Alora, Amphitrite help her, could not move under the intensity of those black eyes.

"You don't remember?" Alora frowned a little. Before they started out, she had thought perhaps the Witch of the Deep and the witch from Grandma Roan's story weren't connected, but now it seemed the only explanation. The Witch of the Deep had to be the same one who had given Grandma Roan her legs. The one who had made a great sacrifice so Grandma Roan could be happy. Otherwise, why would what little magic living in Alora's blood have reacted as it did to her? It had to be magic lingering from the witch's spell—it only made sense that it would rebound as it had.

"Remember what?" The witch sat up fully, her gray brows pulled together, wrinkling the brown skin of her forehead.

"You gave Grandma Roan her legs. Or . . . at least, I think you did." Alora rose so she could sit on the edge of the bed, careful to keep her distance from the witch lest she spook her. And then she relayed the story to her. Of how Grandma Roan's mother had been in love and been lost. Of how Grandma Roan had wished for legs and found love for herself.

When she was finished, the witch had leaned forward, bracing herself with her elbows on her knees. Her eyes were wild, near hidden by a length of gray hair. Her taloned fingers were opening and closing, clutching at air, as if she could capture the memories in her hands but they kept slipping away.

"That was you. I'm sure of it. You gave my Grandma Roan her legs. You . . . you sacrificed something so she could be happy." Alora nodded to herself, certain in her assumptions. There was no other way. And if . . . if this witch had done that for Grandma Roan then she had to be a wonderful, generous creature, even if she didn't remember it. "How can you not remember that?"

"I don't remember anything from the Before." The witch pushed the hair back from her face, finally, her jaw fixing into a tight line.

"The Before?" Alora wrinkled her nose. There was no recognition in the witch's eyes, no realization, and Alora felt her stomach twist. How much had the witch forgotten?

"Before the deep. Before the darkness, and the quiet." The witch shrugged, her shoulders too bony and too pointed in the oversized sweater Alora had dug out of her go-bag. She was swimming in the soft blue fabric, which would be funny in any other situation, but in this situation it made Alora want to reach out to her and wrap her up in her arms.

"How long ago was the Before?"

"I don't know. I sleep a lot." The witch had deflated in on herself it seemed. Her shoulders sagging. Her eyes fixed on where her talons were picking at a loose thread on the blanket.

"All right." Alora nodded, but she was having trouble breathing around an ache that had lodged itself in her throat. What had the witch done to give Grandma Roan happiness? "I guess we'll be learning all of this together then." She forced a smile, lifting her chin. Her *brave face* is what Basanti had always called it, something she pulled on when she felt anything but.

"I suppose . . ." the witch murmured, her gaze still fixed on her lap. Most of her face was hidden by the wild mane of gray hair, but Alora wasn't going to let that bother her. There was work to be done. Mysteries to solve. And what was life without a little mystery? Terribly dull.

"Well, since you're joining the team, we're going to need to know what to call you. We can't just keep calling you the

Witch of the Deep. It's a bit of a mouthful." Alora tilted her head, brushing her own hair behind her ear. "What's your name?"

The witch looked up, her mouth pursed into a hard line, brows drawn together. She looked . . . upset. And for a moment Alora wondered what she had said that was so wrong. But the witch didn't keep her in suspense. "I don't have one."

"What? Of course, you do. Everyone has a name," Alora prodded gently. "Is it something really hard to pronounce? I'm sure I can figure it out if you help me."

"I . . ." The witch stopped, pressing her lips together again and letting out a long breath through her nose. "I think that is what I gave up so your grandmother could be happy. I think I gave up my name."

"Oh." Alora let the word out on a breath as that thing in her chest clenched tighter around her heart. "Oh. That's why Grandma Roan always called you the Witch of the Deep, and never by your name. It's not that she hadn't known it, it's that she —"

"She forgot it. Like everyone else." The witch was staring at Alora again, her black eyes unreadable. "When I gave it up, it was gone forever."

"How do you know that if you don't remember?" Alora frowned.

"I just do." The witch shrugged. "Some things you just know. Like a fish knows to swim."

"Then do you have something you want us to call you?" Alora asked, keeping her voice soft so it wouldn't tremble along with her hands in her lap. The thought of giving up one's name, and how it could erase a person entirely from another's history . . . Of how it could erase them from themselves . . . It shook her.

"No." The witch looked away from Alora, back to the

window. "You were looking for something." Then she scooted back down into the bed and pulled the cover over her head.

"Right." Alora rose slowly, ignoring the way her fingers itched to tug the blankets away and see what exactly the witch was thinking. To try to read her expression and understand her. "I'll just . . . I'll get finished up so you can rest."

## Chapter Six

"*S*arah."

"No." The beast wrinkled her nose and resisted the urge to roll her eyes. They had been at this for what felt like years, and she was tired of Alora's attempts. She was also tired of walking up the Amphitrite-forsaken hill that led to a house that Bimala said belonged to a woman who had provided them information before. A week of hunting down every strange stranger the group had ever worked with had yielded absolutely nothing, and the beast was tired. Tired of these humans. Tired of shoes. Tired of walking. Just tired.

"Susan."

"I don't think so."

"Selene," Alora offered, her green eyes annoyingly bright in her freckled face. The beast winced every time she looked at that ridiculous smiling face; it was too bright, like looking at the sun.

The beast shook her head, which threw off her balance a little, making her wobble.

"What are we talking about?" Basanti asked. She

slowed her pace so she could walk on the other side of Alora.

The rest of their little group was keeping a careful distance from the beast, of which she was grateful. There were too many of them, and they were too loud most of the time. She didn't know if Alora had spoken to them and told them that the beast needed her space, or if they were just afraid of her, but either way she was thankful for the room to breathe. And to stumble foolishly on her still unsure legs.

"We're trying to find a name for her," Alora said. Her hands hovered at her sides, ready at a moment's notice to stop the beast from falling on her face again. The beast thought perhaps if she was another, she might have been touched by such a sentiment — instead, she just found it annoying.

"I thought we were just calling her *the witch*?" Basanti wrinkled her nose daintily. She was a pretty little thing. More minnow than mer. But the beast supposed she could see the beauty in this human. If humans could be called beautiful at all.

"No. We aren't." Alora's mouth ticked down into a frown. She hadn't even bothered to turn her head to look at Basanti, the beast noticed. She focused solely on how the beast was walking. "If you're tired, you need to tell us. We can take a break."

"I'm not weak," the beast bit out, her hands tightening to fists at her sides, unhindered by the talons that cut into her palms. She knew better than to leave blood behind like that, dripping thick and black into the dirt road, but it had been a week and Alora treated her like she was some kind of fragile flower every day. It was infuriating.

"Not weak. Just tired."

*I am tired*, the beast agreed. Being human was exhausting, she had come to realize. Walking was much harder than swimming, the air didn't catch her when she fell like the water did. Then there was the issue of her magic, and how she couldn't use it. She hated it. She hated everything about being human. It was tempting to kill Alora and her group and run back to the water where she would either sink or swim. Or maybe drown. That'd be nice.

"Let's just go." The beast huffed, pushing her legs to work faster so she could outpace Alora and Basanti in spite of the way it made her muscles burn.

"I don't know why we couldn't just take the car." Basanti mumbled under her breath.

"She gets car sick," Alora scolded softly.

"She gets car sick," Basanti repeated in a nasally tone.

The walk up the hill to the house was long, and by the time they got to the top, the beast's feet ached in the shoes they had found for her and she was listing to one side because of a sore on her heel.

Alora moved up beside her, a silent presence, but didn't reach for her. The beast could not decide if she was grateful or annoyed at the gesture. Then she glanced at Alora out of the corner of her eye and decided she was annoyed. *Definitely* annoyed.

"How did we find this person again?" Declan asked, rocking back on his heels. He was a nervous sort, the beast had noticed. The kind of person that, though he was steeped in the world of magic and monsters, seemed completely unsettled by the extraordinary. He fidgeted with the zipper on his jacket until Emrys caught one of his hands with his own and gave it a firm squeeze.

"They've consulted before on some of our early cases." Bimala pressed the bell again, her eyes flicking around them. The beast followed her gaze, taking in the worn bench by the door, discarded shoes with spiders making nests inside stored underneath, the curtain-drawn windows, and the missing beam in the porch. The home was about as well maintained as her own had been.

"This place gives me the creeps," Declan whispered, sliding in closer to Emrys.

*Not as stupid as he looks*, the beast thought idly as the skin on her neck prickled with the traces of magic lingering in the air. Even without access to her own power, she recognized the call of it. Like called to like, after all. Whoever lived in this place wasn't human. Or had visitors who weren't human. The beast wasn't sure which, but the idea put her strangely on edge. She straightened, taking a step closer to the door, putting herself between it and Alora as the magic twisted in the air, the presence it came from moving toward the entrance. She didn't bother to think what the action meant.

"Don't be such a wimp, Declan." Basanti snorted, rolling her eyes. "It's just an old—"

The door creaked open to reveal a small woman with a black lace shawl wrapped tight over her bowed shoulders. Her brown skin was wrinkled, with laugh lines, but she did not look as old as the beast was sure she told people she was, nor as old as she *really* was. And like a strong perfume, the magic wafting off of her hit the beast, making her nose wrinkle.

"Isn't it rude to call your elders old?" she asked, tilting her head to the side. Her eyes narrowed intently on Basanti before they bounced to her twin. "You must be Bimala."

"Yes, ma'am. Thank you for meeting with us." Bimala bowed her head in respect, offering the woman a small smile.

The woman looked her over with a keen eye, and then nodded as if she'd decided something. "You should come in before the rain starts. The roof on the porch leaks."

"Rain? But the forecast said . . ." Emrys blinked, leaning

back over the edge of the porch to get a look at the sky. A moment later, rain started down in a torrent, the air humming with electricity. The beast pressed her lips into a hard line, watching the woman. She hadn't even twitched, but the magic had grown thicker, making it hard for the beast to breathe around it.

"Like I said." The woman met the beast's eyes and hers narrowed for a moment, her lips pursed as if she knew exactly what the beast was. Then she turned to head inside, throwing "The porch leaks" over her shoulder.

A drop landed on the beast's nose and she glared at the woman, watching as the others bustled inside to get away from the weather.

"Shoes off at the door. I'll make some tea."

"Thank you, ma'am. You're very kind." Bimala smiled, already bending to untie her boots. That one was too polite for her own good, the beast was quickly coming to realize.

"Yes. Kind," the beast muttered, refusing to bend to undo her own shoes as she watched the woman over the backs of the others. The woman wasn't looking at her mortal guests. She met the beast's gaze head on, not wavering, and there was something sharp in her eyes. Too sharp for someone playing the part of a feeble old lady.

"Do you need help with the laces?" Alora asked, still crouched, untying her own laces. Then without waiting for an answer, she leaned closer to start helping the beast out of her shoes.

The old woman lifted a brow, her mouth twitching with amusement as her gaze flicked down to Alora, who had already begun to unknot the beast's shoelaces, and the beast could practically hear the mocking tone. Oh, how far the Witch of the Deep hath lowered herself to allow a mortal child to untie her shoelaces.

"I can do it." The beast nudged Alora's fingers away

with her foot, but Alora grabbed them again. "I said I can do it!"

Alora huffed but moved away to focus on her own boots.

"The sitting room is just off to your right. I'll be right with you." The woman's amused gaze didn't move from the beast and Alora, and it burned like a brand across the beast's cheeks. She scoffed, rolling her eyes, and kicked off her shoes without untying them at all. Which earned her an annoyed look from Alora, but she didn't say anything.

They filed into the sitting room, each perching themselves on a piece of dusty, well-worn furniture. The beast didn't think she would ever get used to the unusual softness of human furnishings. She felt like she was sinking down into every sofa she sat on, and it was often a struggle to escape its depths.

When the woman returned, it was with a tray that jingled with too many teacups.

"Here, let me." Emrys rose and swooped in to take it from her before settling it onto the table in front of the sofa. The table wobbled a little on its one uneven leg, but the tea seemed safe enough.

"Thank you again for meeting with us, Miss Bowman." Bimala still had that polite smile plastered onto her face, and the beast wondered if it made her cheeks ache.

"You can call me Arty," the woman said, taking a cup from the tray without offering to pour for anyone else and dropping into a chair with a blanket folded over the arm. Dust motes floated up from the cushion, and it took Arty a moment of shifting before she was finally settled. Then she nodded to the tea tray. "Please. Help yourselves."

The beast watched as the mortals tripped over themselves to pour tea and hand out cups to each other in an effort to look polite. A snort leaving her, she met Arty's gaze again. She wasn't sure what Arty *was*, but she knew what she was *not*, and that was mortal.

"So, what brings you out this far to see me?" Arty tilted her head, sitting her cup down on its saucer. She turned her head to Alora, offering her a soft smile.

"I was cursed a few weeks ago by a woman in white." Alora sat up straighter, setting down her cup so she could tug the collar of her shirt down and show Arty the creeping bruises. They had spread farther since the last time the beast had seen them, painting Alora's collarbone in livid purples. The point of origin of one had flaked away to reveal a bit of hard skin underneath that looked slightly green in the low light. The beast's fingers twitched to tug the shirt away so she could get a better look.

"And this has what to do with the mermaid?" Arty asked, her smile crawling farther up her cheeks, shark-like and jagged.

"How did you know she was a mermaid?" Declan shifted in his seat, leaning toward Arty.

"Every monster knows how to recognize one of their own."

Declan recoiled, ducking behind Emrys's shoulder on the couch. Alora stiffened, her hands tightening to fists in her lap. The twins had gone oddly still, their eyes wide in shock. But the beast sat watching Arty, waiting for her to make a move. Had she brought them all there to feed? Or was she going to help? There was only one way to find out, and that was to wait.

"Relax." Arty scoffed, setting her cup on a side table cluttered in books. "I don't sustain myself on the lives of mortals anymore. Not since . . ." She stopped, her eyes darting to the empty chair beside her, and she shook her head. "Not for long time."

"What are you?" Basanti's eyes had narrowed on Arty,

her gaze calculating as if she could do anything to the old monster. The beast knew better. If Arty wanted to, they would be no match for her, not even with the beast's magic. Whatever Arty was, she was too old and too powerful, and they were in her territory. Even at full strength, the beast would have been no match for her.

"That's not important. What is important is that your friend here is cursed, and your other friend . . . I'm assuming you want your tail back?"

"You can't do that," the beast said, stretching her legs out in front of her to cross at the ankles almost casually, but she saw the way the challenge made Arty's eye twitch. "It has to be the same magic to do the unmaking."

"I'm aware." Arty met the beast in a stare down, a smile playing at the corners of her lips — small, but no less sharp.

"So you'll help us?" Alora broke in, her face so young and eager that it made the beast ache. How could someone who thought she had seen so much be so foolish?

*Don't you know you shouldn't make deals with monsters, girl?*

"I don't see why not." Arty shrugged, picking up her tea again to finish it off. Then she reclined her chair with a loud *thunk*, the springs giving a squeak, and made herself quite comfortable. "Tell me how all of this came about."

# Chapter Seven

"I see," Arty said, leaning farther back in her chair and steepling her fingers in front of her lips. She tapped them once, twice, and then let out a long, rattling breath. "Do you know why she wants the Witch of the Deep's heart specifically?"

"No." Alora shook her head, a frown wrinkling up her nose. The others around her had fallen silent, Bimala's brow wrinkled in thought, Basanti pursing her lips, Declan tapping his fingers along his knee like he was running calculations, and Emrys rubbing at his stubble. But the witch beside her was still, alert, and watching. Her black eyes narrowed on Arty as if she were expecting the woman to leap forward at any moment and try to devour them all whole. Which, Alora supposed, was fair.

"Then perhaps a replacement can be found." Arty hummed to herself. She pressed her lips to her index fingers for a moment, then looked up at Alora with that still-sharp gaze. "Yes, an equivalent exchange should sate whatever hunger she has for power. We may not even have to tell her that the heart doesn't belong to the Witch of the Deep."

"You think that's why she wants her?" Bimala asked. At some point she had pulled out her phone and begun to take notes of the conversation. She was probably recording it too, if Alora knew her at all. And Alora was never more grateful for Bimala's thoroughness than she was right then.

The witch had gone very still beside Alora, and she itched to reach over and take her hand. To provide some kind of comfort in the face of all that Arty was saying, but she knew the touch would be unwelcome.

"It's an educated guess." Arty shrugged, her hands falling back into her lap. "You can never really know why creatures do things. We don't exactly follow human logic."

"So how do we find this equivalent exchange?" Declan leaned forward, his eyes wide and interested. For someone deathly afraid of getting eaten, he always seemed to be excited by the next big adventure. Alora didn't think she'd ever understand it. But then, she didn't have to—she hadn't married him.

"We need to find a creature who has taken as many lives as the Witch of the Deep. Exactly as many."

"Why not more? Wouldn't one who'd taken more be more powerful?" Basanti tilted her head, dark hair falling into her eyes.

"Yes. But then it might overpower her." Arty pushed herself from her chair, leaning back to stretch out her back a little. "Follow me."

Alora went to push to her feet, but a sharp tug on her sweater stopped her. She looked down, finding the witch's fingers fisted in the fabric, her black eyes following Arty suspiciously as the old woman made her way to the door into the main hall. Alora had to breathe through the desire to wrap the witch in her arms and hide her away from whatever was scaring her. It would be unproductive, and it would likely push the witch further away.

"What for?" the witch asked, her eyes narrowed.

"To find another monster," Arty said, disinterested. "Unless you're willing to give up your heart to save some mortal you just met?"

Alora's eyes drifted down to where the witch was still clutching at her sweater. The witch's black eyes followed her gaze. She released her hold too quickly, like the soft fabric had burned her talons, and jerked her head back up to Arty.

"I didn't think so." Arty turned and headed through the doorway. "Come. Come. We don't have much time."

"Do you have a database of monsters?" Bimala asked, flying from her seat to follow after Arty. Alora rolled her eyes; leave it to Bimala to be excited about the prospect of research.

The others filtered out after Arty, leaving Alora rooted to the spot beside the witch.

"I'm not going to let her have you." Alora stared at the doorway where the others had disappeared, refusing to meet the witch's gaze. That protectiveness she'd felt the first time she'd seen the witch looking so small reared its head again. She knew it was stupid. The witch had killed people. Lots of people. But Alora couldn't seem to swallow down the feeling.

The witch scoffed and rose from her seat. She didn't look back at Alora, but she paused in the threshold, her weight unevenly balanced between her feet. She'd been listing left all day, and Alora wondered if the shoes were bothering her.

"Worry about yourself," the witch said in an almost disgusted tone, then she followed the others down the hall.

Alora leaned back into the hard cushion of the sofa, her hands moving to drag down over her face as she let out a long breath.

"You need to stop." Basanti's voice was soft, but no less chiding for the quiet of it. Alora hadn't noticed her waiting on the other side of the doorframe, but it would seem Basanti had overhead enough of their conversation to have an Opinion about it.

"I know," Alora said from behind her hands. She did know. She knew better than anyone how this was going to end.

"When this is all over, she's going to go back to the sea, and you're going to—"

"I said I *know*, Basanti." Alora smacked her hands down onto her thighs so she could glare at Basanti in the doorway. She knew her friend was just trying to help. She knew that Basanti didn't mean anything by it. There might be a little jealousy behind her words, but most of it was genuine concern for what the witch would leave behind when she left.

"What's with you two, anyway?" Basanti crossed her arms over her chest, her nose wrinkling.

"I don't know what you mean." Alora pushed to her feet, vowing to put this strange feeling that had curled up like a sleeping cat in her chest from her mind. There were other things to worry about, like the patch of cold green-gray skin that the flaking bruise had revealed. She didn't know what she was turning into, but she knew it was something . . . else. Something not human.

"You do." Basanti moved to block her path. "You've been . . ." Basanti waved her hand as if that would make her words make more sense and then she let out an annoyed huff. "Orbiting around each other since we pulled her from that net. It's like she's the damn sun."

"I don't know what you mean," Alora repeated, bumping her shoulder against Basanti's on her way into the hall.

"Fine. Be that way. But I'm not going to be here to pick up the pieces. Not like last time." Basanti let the words hang in the air between them, and Alora decided to pretend she didn't hear them. It would be better, she thought, than to acknowledge the truth in them. Besides, if she acknowledged the truth then she'd have to *think* about the last time. About how that creature had tricked her. About how it had nearly taken a piece of her with it when it — No. No. She was not going to think about that.

THE GROUP SETTLED into Arty's extensive library as they would in any other. Alora would've been impressed by their single-minded focus, but she saw it for what it was: a way to avoid the awkwardness that had sprouted up between herself, the witch, and Basanti. Which was fine, she told herself, it wasn't any of their business anyway.

They worked late into the night, compiling a list of ancient creatures that might act as a good replacement for the witch. And when everyone had begun to flag, Arty offered them rooms, leaving herself and Alora amongst the dusty tomes.

"Your team is very competent," Arty said, her fingers tracing a line of text in a book that looked like it weighed more than she did.

"We should be, we've been doing this long enough." Alora didn't have to look up from where she'd found a text on a kraken to feel Arty's gaze fixed on her.

"You have something you want to ask me."

Alora wasn't sure how she knew. Maybe it had been the way Alora had shifted in her seat as they plowed through book after book. Or maybe it was the way she'd been quiet and thoughtful, more so than any of the others. Either way, Arty had sensed it.

"Now would be the time to do it, if it's something you don't want your friends to hear."

"Do you know what I'm becoming?" The question had weighed heavy on her tongue for days. She'd done her own research, of course, but she hadn't found anything. And without access to the help of her friends, she was left to try to figure it out on her own. She wasn't as good at that as Bimala and Basanti were. That's why they were the team researchers.

"You're worried you'll hurt them." Arty shut the book in her lap and fixed her attention on Alora.

But Alora refused to look up from her own tome to meet her eyes. She didn't think she had it in her to look the truth in the face. She didn't even have the courage to voice her agreement to the question. She just nodded.

"You might hurt them," Arty said, honestly.

"What should I do?" The words left her on a breath, and she clutched the pages in front of her till they wrinkled in her grasp. She felt . . . lost. She needed someone to tell her what to do. How to fix this.

Arty was quiet so long that Alora thought maybe she wouldn't answer, the tension between them stretching and stretching to near snapping.

"If this doesn't work. If we can't find someone to go in the witch's place, what should I do?" Alora forced the words out. They scraped the whole way up, like broken glass.

"In the end . . ." Arty said, her tone measured. Alora could see her wrinkled hands where they had tightened into fists on top of the book she was holding. Alora looked up to meet Arty's deep brown eyes. They were glassy, like Arty had begun to cry and swallowed it back. Like she understood, perhaps better than anyone, the price that Alora would ultimately have to pay, the feelings she had thus far been unable to explain. "In the end, you're going to have to make a choice. Her life, or yours."

"And if I can't?"

"Can't or won't?"

"And if I won't?" Alora amended, ducking her head to look down at her own hands. She'd bitten her fingernails to the quick at some point over the last few days to try to keep herself focused, and to keep her hands from straying too much to the witch. The witch, who had made it clear that she was going home when this was done. That she wanted nothing to do with Alora. That she didn't feel the same draw that Alora had since the moment they'd first locked eyes.

"Inaction is also a choice." Arty nodded, a soft, tired smile taking over her voice.

"What happens if I go through with it?" Alora knew she wasn't going to before she'd even spoken the words, but she had to know. She had to fully understand everything before she could choose whose life was more important. Hers or the witch's. "What happens if I give the woman in white her heart?"

"Then she ceases to be."

"So she dies." Alora's stomach sank. She had known that, of course she had. Even monsters needed their hearts to exist. And if Alora cut out the witch's, of course it would kill her.

"No. She ceases to exist."

"What's the difference?" Alora frowned, her eyes flicking back up to meet Arty's. The old woman was staring at her intently, as if she could impart some wisdom through the gaze. As if she could make Alora understand something that Alora had no hope of grasping. And then Alora remembered the empty chair, and the extra pair of slippers by the door that had gathered dust, and she thought maybe she understood.

"If she dies, she'll be reincarnated. But if the woman in white gets her heart, her power? She'll no longer exist. That will be the end of the Witch of the Deep." Arty was staring at Alora, her gaze steady, her words soft. It didn't lessen the blow, however much she might have tried.

"Wouldn't that be better?" The words left Alora's lips, but she didn't know exactly where they'd come from. Especially as they didn't sound like her at all. But something cold had gripped her chest, like icy fingers. "She's killed people. Thousands. Wouldn't it be better if she didn't exist?"

"You don't mean that." Arty frowned, the wrinkles on her face shifting to something sad, and tired.

Alora sucked in a breath and the fingers released, her body tingling with warmth again. "I don't," she agreed.

"You need to be careful saying things you don't mean." Arty stood from her chair, setting the book aside. "Words have power. Especially names," Arty added almost absently. "With what you do, you should know that better than anyone."

"Right. I'm sorry." Alora ducked her head, her shoulders hunching forward.

Arty shook her head. "Just . . . be more careful. And get some rest." She moved to pat Alora's shoulder, her hand oddly strong for a woman of her age. "You're going to need it."

"All right." Alora nodded and let Arty go without another word before turning back to her book.

# Chapter Eight

"*You're* coming with us?" Alora asked in a tone that said she wasn't so sure it was a good idea, and honestly, the beast agreed. She didn't trust Arty, even for all the help she'd provided them so far. But then, the beast thought it was bad practice to trust anyone whose true face you couldn't see.

"That is what it looks like, isn't it?" Arty's tone was mocking as she hitched the bag she'd packed farther up her shoulder. The beast thought perhaps one of them should offer to help her with it, but she wasn't going to be the first to do so. Not if not helping would deter Arty from coming along.

"Aren't you a little old to be monster hunting? You've got to be at least eighty." Basanti snorted. Bimala nudged her and shot her a reproachful look, but Basanti just shrugged her off. "What? She is."

"Come, child, let me teach you a thing or two about monster hunting." Arty held out her hand to Basanti. When Basanti stepped forward, Arty looped her arm around Basanti's shoulders and pulled the taller woman down to her level. "Never ask a monster her age." She flicked Basanti in the forehead. "We'll take my car down the hill to where you parked."

"Where are we headed?" Emrys had one of those little black devices called a phone out and was typing away on it, his fingers flying in quick motions the beast didn't think she'd ever get used to.

"Scotland," Alora said, stepping out onto the porch. She turned, her hand twitching at her side like maybe she was going to offer to help the beast down the stairs, but she didn't bother. The beast frowned a little, scrubbing her palm against her thigh when it itched to reach back.

Emrys nodded. "I'll book us a flight —"

"No." Alora shook her head. "I don't think the witch is ready to get on a plane. We'll take the train."

The beast's eyes flicked to Alora, who was looking everywhere but at the beast.

Arty let out a soft, amused sound but said nothing more on the subject, and they were off.

"CHARLOTTE. VIOLET. HAZEL. OH! I KNOW!" Alora snapped her fingers. She had been listing names for at least a full hour at that point, and the beast wasn't sure how to get her to stop. Everyone else had filtered out of the little room on the train, citing some excuse like needing the bathroom, or heading to the dining car. Leaving Alora and the beast alone. "Luna."

The beast sighed loudly, smacking her head back against the seat, and closed her eyes. She didn't know how much more she could take of Alora's insistence that they find her a name. Couldn't Alora see that she didn't *want* a name? All she wanted to do was go home. Back to the dark and the quiet and the death that waited for her somewhere in the not-so-far-off future.

"Are you just naming all the women you've been with?" the beast asked, though she wasn't sure where the question had really come from. She didn't know enough about Alora to make the assumption that Alora preferred women, but she'd seen the way Basanti watched her. Seen the way Basanti's eyes clung to Alora like nettles when she thought Alora wasn't looking. There had been something there, not so long ago, and that was enough of an indication in the beast's book. And besides, maybe if she could shock Alora into shutting up, she could get some rest.

"What? No!" Alora laughed, shaking her head so that a lock of red hair fell into her eyes. "I wouldn't do that."

"Then stop listing names off without first thinking about if they even fit me." The beast tsked, rolling her eyes. "Honestly, it's like you don't even care."

"That's not true." Alora leaned forward, taking one of the beast's hands in her own and giving it a squeeze.

The beast blinked down at where Alora's light-brown skin brushed over the slowly fading talons of her hand. She didn't know when they had started to fade away. When she had started to look more mortal. But the nails that had previously shredded any fabric they came into contact with had become blunt. And the spill of ink-black magic that had been crawling up her fingertips since before she could remember was bleeding away the longer Alora touched her skin, sharing her warmth with the beast. The beast jerked her hand away and sat back in her seat to stare out the window, arms crossed.

"Right. Sorry." Alora scrubbed at her nose, sitting back as well, a look of hurt pinched between her brows. "It's weird. I feel like I know you."

"You don't." How could she? Alora was so young, and

the beast had been around for so long. They didn't know each other. But . . .

"I know that, but I feel like I do."

*I do too*, the beast didn't say. Because what point would there be? What would it change? Nothing. She rolled onto her side and curled the hood of the oversized sweater Alora had loaned her up over her head to block out the light. "I'm going to sleep."

Time ticked away after that, and the beast lost track of it. She laid there with the hood over her head, breathing into the darkness of the fabric and ignoring the sounds of movement around her. Because she didn't care. She didn't. The mortals could be marching off to their death, and that was fine.

The train stopped. The mortals gathered their belongings. There was some minor argument over who should wake her, and then she felt someone shake her shoulder lightly, warmth bleeding from their fingertips into the fabric.

"It's time to go," Alora whispered, her voice soft and kind. "Take your time getting up, though. Declan and Emrys are loading the car."

"I'm fine." The beast shrugged her off and sat up, ignoring the way the room seemed to spin when she moved too quickly. She was not some fragile thing to be pitied.

"Of course, you are," Alora snapped, her words brittle and cold. And then she cleared her throat and straightened up. "I'll be outside."

The beast watched her go, her head tilted to the side. She had never heard Alora's voice like that. It hadn't been long, granted, but Alora seemed incapable of being that unfeeling when it wasn't deserved. There was something wrong with her. Something that wasn't on the surface. Something she wasn't showing the others. The beast shook herself and rose to her feet, taking a steadying breath to ready for the long car ride to wherever they were going. She didn't think she'd ever get used to that particular mode of travel.

"Where to first?" Emrys asked when everyone had loaded up into the oversized vehicle they had rented. The beast thought Bimala had called it a *van*, but she couldn't be sure.

"The inn is by the lake. There's no sense in heading out on the boat until this evening anyway." Arty had somehow ranked above the others and gotten the seat beside Emrys. She looked smug about it as the others squeezed themselves into the back of the vehicle. The beast clicked her tongue in annoyance and looked back out the window.

"Are we going to catch Nessie?" Declan asked, leaning forward so he could poke his head in between Alora and the beast. The beast had the urge to shove him back by his face, but she kept it in check.

"We aren't going to Loch Ness." Bimala scoffed. "So, no. We aren't going to get Nessie."

"Besides, Nessie has been debunked, remember?" Basanti asked. "That one was . . ."

"Not me." Alora shook her head. "I never bothered with Nessie. Grandpa Jiro, Uncle Milo, and Grandma Roan looked into it back in the day."

The chatter faded into the background as the beast's mind stuck on those names. Jiro. Roan. She knew them. She didn't know where she knew them from. But she knew them. They lingered somewhere in the distance. Not out of sight, but out of reach. The beast closed her eyes, trying to push for the memories, and hissed when a throbbing pain jabbed into her temple.

"Are you all right?" someone asked, but their voice sounded like it was coming through water. All muffled and indistinct. The beast opened her eyes, and even her eyesight was watery, but she could see the smudge of Alora's red hair as the other woman leaned in to check on the beast. "Stop the car, I think she's getting car sick again."

"We're almost there. Can't she hang on?" Emrys called back.

"I'm fine!" The beast shrugged Alora off, taking a deep breath to quell the sick feeling rising in the back of her throat as her vision swam. "I'm fine!"

Awkward tension rippled through the vehicle, but the others stayed out of it.

"Fine. You're fine." Alora nodded, sitting back in her seat.

SOMEONE WAS KNOCKING at the beast's door and all she could do was pray it wasn't Alora. She didn't have the energy to deal with that at the moment; they hadn't even been at the inn a couple of hours, and she needed a break from all the mortals and their . . . *emotions*. She thought to ignore the knock, but that would only make them worry. So she rose and opened the door.

"You're pushing yourself too hard," Arty said, brushing past her into the room without even a nod of greeting.

"I don't know what you're talking about." The beast glared at the short woman, wishing her irritated gaze were enough to get Arty to leave her alone. It wasn't. But it was always worth a try.

"You can't remember how you got to be this way, can you?" Arty moved to sit on the edge of the beast's bed. Her eyes were narrowed on the beast, inspecting.

"What does it matter?"

"Something Alora said triggered a memory," Arty

continued, not answering the question. Amphitrite help her, how had the beast wound up with such meddlesome company? Maybe this was her true punishment for whatever she'd done in her past. Not all those years in the dark, but these annoying people. "Don't go chasing something you willingly sacrificed."

"Why not?" The beast crossed her arms over her chest, leaning against the still-open door to her room. She hoped that leaving it open would hint to Arty that she needed to leave, but the old monster seemed quite content to make herself at home. The beast felt her eye twitch.

"Because you can't get it back. No matter what you do, you can't get it back. All you can do is stay and make new memories for yourself. Try to find a new happiness."

"What are you, an oracle?" The beast snorted, rolling her eyes, but it did little to cover the way Arty's words made her insides writhe with . . . something. Some kind of emotion the beast was sure she'd never felt. New memories. New happiness. As if she could ever find those things here, of all places. "I don't need my fortune told, old monster. Now get out and let me rest."

"Don't say I didn't warn you." Arty shrugged. "I came up to let you know that it's time to go. The others have already grabbed their gear. We're just waiting on you."

"I don't need to go with them."

Arty scoffed, dropping back onto her feet and heading to the door. "Don't come crying to me if that thing drowns your friends."

"They're not my *friends*." The beast clicked her tongue in annoyance. But she was already dragging the hooded shirt down over her head again and clomping to the door in her borrowed boots.

"Sure they aren't."

## Chapter Nine

The night was clear, the moon reflecting off the still waters of the lake. There was no indication at all that the lake had been the site of many a gruesome drowning. No hint of blood on the air. No dying screams lingering on the faint breeze. If Alora didn't know any better, she'd think the place looked idyllic and restful. The perfect setting for a work retreat or a writers' workshop, something that required spotty cell coverage and lots of quiet.

"Do you really think there's anything here?" Declan asked, his voice creeping up into the higher octaves.

Alora did her best to keep from rolling her eyes, but it was a struggle. She didn't know why Declan had even come. He could have stayed behind at the inn where it was safe and there was a roaring fire in the hearth. Instead, he was wrapped tightly in a loud yellow raincoat and shivering against a nonexistent chill. *Coward*.

"There have been too many mysterious deaths on this lake for it to be a coincidence." Bimala's eyes were fixed on the soft glow of her phone screen. Even with the brightness turned all the way down, she was squinting against the glare.

"Yeah, but you said it's been a couple of years. Maybe it's moved on?" Declan's voice was muffled from where he'd pressed his face into Emrys's shoulder. His eyes squeezed shut to hide from something that hadn't even appeared yet.

"No. It's still here." Arty's voice was soft, barely above a whisper, but it seemed to echo across the water.

The witch had moved to lean over the side of the boat, staring down into the depths as though she could see something the others couldn't. Maybe she could. Arty had said that one monster always recognized another.

"Turn it off," the witch ordered, voice quiet but hard.

"What?" Basanti frowned, her hands gripping the wheel harder. "We're not even a quarter of the way in—"

"It's watching us." The witch didn't look away from the water, but Alora could see her shoulders tighten. "Turn it off."

"What?" Declan squeaked.

"How do you know?" Emrys's eyes had narrowed on the witch, suspicion lacing his features.

"Can't you feel it?" Arty moved to stand beside the witch, her eyes fixed to the same spot where the witch's black gaze had settled.

"Do what she says." Alora's hands clenched at her sides. There was the need again, like a wriggling under her skin, to be close to the witch. To make sure she was all right, at the very least. A protective, incessant feeling curling around her veins and making it hard for Alora to think.

Basanti grumbled under her breath, but when Alora turned to glare at her, she cut the engine. Without the growl of the motor, there was only the stillness of the lake and the sounds of life coming from Alora's team.

"I don't hear anything," Declan whispered.

Alora couldn't either, but she could feel it. The faint hum in the air that seemed to buzz along her skin, lifting the hairs on her arms and making a shiver run down her spine. The witch was right—something was watching them. A predator eyeing its prey. The feeling grew stronger and stronger until Alora wasn't sure how the others couldn't feel it; it was almost audible.

"What is that?" Bimala asked, her fingers gripping the phone in her hand hard enough that she was accidentally pressing the buttons on the side, the screen washing her face in ghostly pale light.

"We need to leave," the witch said, her voice sharp. The tension in her back had tightened, dragging her boney shoulders up to her ears. Her jaw was clenched so hard that Alora could see the muscle ticking beneath the skin.

"Why?" Basanti snorted. Alora could hear the eye roll in her tone, but her gaze was locked on the witch.

Arty had gone oddly still beside her.

Something knocked against the bottom of the boat, like they'd run over a log, and the witch jerked back, her head whipping around to look at Alora with wide, fearful eyes. "Now! We have to go *now*!"

Alora spun, her feet already moving to take the wheel from Basanti. But it was too late. It was much too late. Whatever had been watching them had decided it didn't want to wait any longer. The boat rocked dangerously, almost throwing Arty from it. Alora's knees nearly gave out at the jolt, but the witch was right. They needed to leave.

Another bump, and Alora swore the boat nearly tipped onto its side. She reached the wheel in enough time to pry it from Basanti's white-knuckled grasp and kick the engine on. She turned the key, and it clicked, clicked, clicked, then sputtered, then shut off again.

She turned it again, holding on for dear life as the creature nearly capsized them again.

"Alora," Basanti said, voice shaking.

"I know. I know. I'm trying!" The engine whined like a dying animal, half drowned and gasping for breath. "Start! Start, you stupid thing! Start!"

"What the hell is that?" Emrys shrieked, but Alora didn't have time to look up and find out what he was talking about. They needed to get out of there. They needed to get back to shore. Before the damn thing drowned them all. Screw her curse. Screw the woman in white. She wasn't going to lose her friends!

"Alora." Basanti's hands gripped her sleeve so tight that Alora could feel her nails scraping her skin through the fabric.

"I'm trying, Basanti! I'm trying!" Alora's voice cracked on the words, panic and tears threatening to choke them off where she forced them out. Her hand started shaking on the key, but she turned it over again, the engine not even bothering to make more than a pathetic groan this time.

"No. Look."

Alora looked up to follow Basanti's trembling finger and found the huge skeletal head of something poking out from below the surface. She couldn't make out if it was a reptile or a mammal, but that didn't seem to matter. Because most of its face was swallowed up by glassy black eyes, like one of those ridiculous alien cartoons. And reflected in their depths was the witch. The witch tilted her head, and the creature mimicked the motion.

The water around them had stilled, calming so that the boat was rocking gently in the waves the creature had made. Then, like a spell broke, the creature reached for the witch. Long fingers with too many joints wrapped all the way around her waist and yanked her forward over the rail of the boat.

"No!" Alora shook Basanti loose and rushed across the slick floor of the boat, her shoes skidding. By the time she reached the side, there was but a ripple where the witch had disappeared beneath the black water. Alora didn't wait. She didn't think. She braced her foot on the slippery metal railing and lunged over the edge to follow the witch into the depths, ignoring the screams of her team.

The water was cold and dark around her. She squeezed her eyes shut hard and opened them again, but there was still no light to see by. Just the black. Gritting her teeth, Alora pushed herself to the surface to suck in a deep breath and dive back in, kicking toward the lake floor. But there was nothing to follow. No sign of the witch or the monster.

And then Alora remembered what Arty had told her. Words had power. Names especially. And she thought of a name that had been sitting on her tongue for weeks now, the one she had been afraid to speak for fear the witch would shake it off as she had so many others. A name that had lingered at the back of Alora's mind since she was a little girl. The one she'd used for a teddy bear, an imaginary friend, and even her first goldfish. A name that was so engrained in her, she didn't know how it hadn't been the first she'd offered the witch.

Kicking back to the surface, Alora took another lungful of air.

"Alora! What the hell are you doing?" Basanti screamed from the boat. It sounded like they had gotten the engine started again, but that was background noise to the feeling of that name humming like a live wire under her skin.

"Eos!" Alora shouted the name into the night, and then there was light. A glowing red string of it burning like a brand through the black water. It tied in a knot around her ring finger and disappeared into the current. Alora took another breath and dove, following the string.

It led her to the witch. The glow revealed a slack mouth and heavy-lidded black eyes. There was no creature in sight. Alora grabbed the witch by the waist and pulled her back to the surface, her legs burning from the strain of her clothes weighing her down.

"Help me get her up!" she called to the others when she finally broke the surface and started toward the boat again.

Emrys and Declan hauled the witch onto the boat while Basanti and Bimala helped Alora. Arty was watching the whole process with keen eyes, but Alora didn't have time to deal with that, not yet.

"She's not breathing, Alora." Declan had leaned forward to listen to the witch's chest, and what he heard left him looking stricken. "What should I do? Will CPR even work?"

"Get out of my way." Alora scrambled over to the witch's side, brushing her gray hair away from her face. "Breathe," she pleaded. Her fingers trembled where they brushed the witch's brown skin.

"Breathe, Eos!" The words came out a command, and Alora's skin prickled, her fingers glowing softly as they had that first time she'd touched the witch and turned her human. "Breathe, damn it!"

The witch sucked in a hard breath, gasping, rasping, choking on it. Alora turned her onto her side so the witch could cough up the black water she'd pulled into her lungs. And when she was done, she turned bleary black eyes on Alora. "What did you call me?"

"Eos." A smile twitched at the corner of Alora's lips, tentative and shy.

"So that's my name," the witch—no, Eos—said almost absently.

"It is?" Declan asked, his head cocked.

"Mm-hmm." Eos nodded, and hope bloomed in Alora's chest, warming the space where the woman in white had left her mark behind. "It is."

"Well, that's wonderful. But we need to get out of here before that thing gets hungry again," Basanti said, breaking the moment.

"I don't think he'll be bothering us anymore tonight." Eos's voice was still raspy from all the water she'd coughed up, and she sounded tired.

"Be that as it may," Arty said, turning to nod at Basanti, who had returned to the wheel. "We need to get you two into some dry clothes."

"And you should rest," Alora added, fingers lingering perhaps too long to brush more of the hair away from where it stuck to Eos's forehead. The gesture was so soft and affectionate, she was sure Eos would push her away. But she didn't. Instead, Eos seemed to lean into the warmth of Alora's hands, and Alora couldn't fight back a smile.

"Yes. Rest." Eos let her eyes flutter closed again, but Alora found relief in the subtle shift of her chest as she took in deep breaths.

The engine grumbled to life, and Basanti steered them back to shore.

## Chapter Ten

os.

      Eos.

Eos.

The beast turned the name over and over in her head. It wasn't her original name, the one her mother had gifted her with when she'd been born all those years ago, she knew that. But it felt oddly right. It fit like a freshly tailored tunic. Or what she imagined a freshly tailored tunic would fit like. New, but no less right.

"What does it mean?" Eos asked, tugging her blanket more firmly around her shoulders. She had never felt cold before. The ocean had always seemed warm despite its depths. But here on land, she was constantly reminded how a chill could easily settle into her human skin. It was strange.

"Hm?" Alora hummed in question. She was listing to one side, looking groggy and a little green about the gills.

"Eos. What does it mean?"

"Eos was the Greek goddess of the dawn. It means . . . a new beginning."

"Greek?"

"Mm-hmm." Alora nodded, her eyes going a little glassy. She blinked hard and focused on Eos again. "Grandpa Jiro loved Greek mythology. He taught us all about it before he passed, and I did a dissertation on it when I got my doctorate."

Eos frowned thoughtfully, her focus going back to the fire. The others had wrapped them up in blankets and deposited them in the two wingback chairs in front of the fireplace of the little inn's sitting room. Then they'd gone off to . . . Well, Eos didn't really know what they'd gone off to do. Something about research, and interviews, whatever that meant. Arty had grunted that she was going to bed. Which was likely where Eos and Alora should be . . .

Alora winced, clutching her chest, her head thunking against the chair back. Eos jerked half out of her chair to reach for Alora.

"What is it? What's wrong?" Eos pushed the words out on a quick breath, hands scrambling to grip Alora's shoulders and keep her from falling out of her own chair.

"It hurts," Alora hissed through clenched teeth. Her face had gone very pale.

"What hurts?"

Alora clawed at the blanket Declan had wrapped tightly around her, tugging it down away from her neck to reveal the slow crawl of the woman in white's mark making its way up Alora's throat. It turned the skin discolored then dry, and Alora's nails scraped over it, clawing away the layer of skin on top to reveal leathery green beneath.

"Stop scratching at it," Eos growled, grabbing Alora's wrist to pry her fingers away when the nails had gone bloody.

"It burns."

Eos's fingers brushed over the skin, hoping to soothe it

with her own cool touch. She yelped, jerking back when the biting cold of it seeped the warmth from her fingertips. "Amphitrite, you're freezing."

"Burns." Alora's voice quivered, her body beginning to shiver. It was still spreading, the mark bleeding up toward her chin.

"We've got to get you warmed up." Eos wrapped the blanket tighter around Alora, pulling her into her chest. "We've just got to get you warmed up. That'll stop it. That'll slow it down."

She wasn't sure who she was trying to reassure—Alora or herself—but she didn't suppose it mattered. Not right then. Not as Alora let out a soft shuddering breath, the air puffing cold against Eos's cheek. "Eos."

"I know." Eos frowned down at the still spreading mark. It had slowed, but not stopped. Creeping like ink through still water.

"You need to get her in a bath." The voice broke Eos's focus on the mark, and she looked up to see Arty beside them. "The quicker we bring her body temperature up, the quicker it stops."

"But the fire—"

"It's not enough. Do you think you can stand, child?"

Alora looked up at Arty through bleary, unfocused eyes, and nodded weakly.

"Let me help you." Eos pulled Alora slowly to her feet, looping her arm over her shoulders.

Alora stumbled a little, but Eos tugged her in close by a tight arm around her waist and supported as much of her weight as her weak human legs could hold. It would be easier with a tail, she thought in passing. She'd always been stronger with a tail. The stairs were a struggle, but somehow Eos managed to get herself and Alora up them and to the little bathroom off her room.

"Don't turn the fan on," Arty ordered, moving to the tub to turn a knob on the wall. Water poured from the spout, beginning to fill up the little tub. "We need the steam."

"The what?" Eos blinked at Arty.

"Never mind. Just get her out of that blanket."

"Cold." Alora whined as Eos carefully unwound the blanket from her shoulders. There was blood where it had pressed against the open wound on her neck, slowly dying the white fuzz red. "So cold."

"I know. I know it's cold. But we're going to get you warmed up, I promise." Eos dropped the blanket to the floor and moved with Alora to the tub where Arty was crouched, checking the temperature.

Alora screamed, her head falling forward as the mark spread faster, like a burn, racing up along her jaw.

"Quick, before it gets into her lungs." Arty pushed Eos to the edge, and she stepped over, ignoring the way the water burned at her skin and soaked the bottoms of her pants through. "Easy does it."

Eos held Alora's waist tightly, helping her stumble into the tub, and then lowered her carefully into the water at her feet. She braced her back against Eos's shins.

Alora released a breath, a sigh, her lids fluttering heavily.

"Move her hair, so we can see if it's working."

Eos's fingers moved softly against the skin of Alora's cheek, brushing away the clinging hair. The mark had crept up to the hinge in Alora's jaw, but it had stopped. One tendril of it crawled up farther, nearly touching her ear, but it was no longer burning its way through her skin. It had left its traces across the whole left side of her throat, leaving some skin cracked, some mottled like a bruise, and a big section turned green and leathery.

"It's stopped." Eos slumped against the tile wall of the shower stall.

"For now." Arty stood, stretching out her back. Alora's eyes had fallen shut, her back heavy and wet where it pressed into Eos's legs.

"What *was* that?"

"She used magic to save you. It sped up the change." Arty reached over to turn off the water before it could spill over the edge onto the floor. "Keep her in here a bit, just to make sure we've warded off the chill."

"That'll keep it from spreading?"

"No. But it'll keep it from speeding up again. We have to keep her warm."

Eos nodded. Her fingers fell to stroke through Alora's hair, brushing it back from her face again almost mindlessly. "How much longer does she have?"

"I don't know. A month maybe? The woman in white gave her till the blood moon, but with this . . ." Arty shook her head.

Eos slumped, her eyes fixed on the patch of gray-green skin on Alora's neck.

"Well. Now that that's taken care of, I'm going back to bed."

Eos blinked, lifting her gaze to watch as the old woman all but hobbled out of the bathroom. She half thought to tell Arty to cut the act, that none of the humans were looking, but then decided not to bother. There wasn't any point anyway. Arty would do what she wanted.

When she was gone, Eos looked down at Alora and let out a long sigh. Alora was breathing easier, her chest rising and falling at a steady pace instead of the quickened one like before. And each breath wasn't hitched with pain. In fact, Eos half wondered if she'd fallen asleep.

"Towels," Eos told herself, shifting to step out of the tub

to get things ready so Alora wouldn't feel chilled when they left the tub.

Alora's hand shot out, grabbing Eos's forearm in a grip that was too strong for a woman who had been so weak a few minutes ago. "Not yet. Stay a little longer."

"You need dry clothes."

"In a little." Alora gave Eos's arm a sharp tug, and her knees buckled under the force of it. "Stay. Tell me a story."

Alora leaned forward, and Eos let herself sink down behind her, water seeping into her sweater. She bent her knees on either side of Alora's hips as Alora leaned back into her.

"I don't know any stories."

"Then tell me something else. A memory. Something that made you smile. Something that made you sad. Just . . . something." Alora's voice had gone fuzzy and tired around the edges. Like she was half-asleep already. Eos supposed it didn't matter what she told her.

"I think there was a girl I loved once," Eos said, her voice just louder than the soft lap of the water in the tub from when they'd shifted. "Someone I gave up everything for, even my name."

"Think?" Alora tipped her head back to look up at Eos's chin.

"Well, I must have. Otherwise, why did I become like this?"

"Who was she?" Alora took her hand, pulling it in front of her so she could run her fingertip up the length of one very human finger. It felt strangely familiar, and it made Eos's heart stutter a little in her chest.

"I don't remember." Eos let out a breath, hoping Alora wouldn't hear the way it hitched with unshed tears. "I just know that I was hers, and she was mine. And in the end, it wasn't enough."

"That's sad."

"Is it?" Eos cleared her throat, jerking her eyes away from where Alora was now running her thumb along her palm. "I wish I knew."

They sat in silence for a long while, the water slowly cooling, and the brush of Alora's fingers over the pads of Eos's thumb, her knuckles, her wrist, calmed Eos. Let her racing heart slow. Brought her peace.

Eos's mind wandered, the creature's dark eyes flashing across her memory. The way she had seen her reflection in their depths. The way she had seen herself in it. "What if it's not killing because it wants to?"

"What?" Alora asked, her voice lazy with sleep.

"The creature in the lake," Eos clarified. "What if it's not killing because it wants to?"

"Then why would it—"

"What if it's killing because it's hurting? What if it's killing because it knows grief, and pain, and loss? What if it's—" Eos choked on the words she'd only half thought all the way through. "What if it's just like me?"

Alora sat up, the water lapping against the tub as she turned herself around and took Eos's face into her hands. Her palms were calloused, Eos noted distantly, and slick with warm water.

"You didn't become a monster by choice," she said with such certainty that Eos thought maybe she could feel it down to the very marrow of her bones. Almost believed it, even. Alora's eyes had cleared. Her brows pinched together like something had finally clicked into place. Like something was finally making sense. "You gave up your memories for my Grandma Roan. So she could be human."

Eos blinked, her teeth gnawing on the inside of her cheek. She had no recollection of that, but it sounded like the truth. It felt like the truth.

"You did it to make someone else happy." Alora's wrinkled fingertips brushed hair away from Eos's face where it clung to her temples, and Eos found herself leaning into the warmth of Alora's touch, as foolish as she knew it was.

"People make choices every day, Alora. And in the end, that was a choice. One that I made willingly."

"It's not the same." Alora shook her head and wobbled a little with the motion as if she were dizzy from it.

"Isn't it?" She knew it was. Eos had no doubts that she'd become a monster with gladness. That it had made her happy, at least in the moment, to give herself up to see another live out their dream. "Either way, we can't punish the creature for hurting."

"No . . . No, we can't." Alora's fingers clutched at Eos's cheeks almost painfully. "Whatever we do, it'll have to be humane."

"You mean put it out of its misery?" Eos snorted to cover a flash of something like a bullet wound to her chest, and she jerked her face out of Alora's hold so she didn't have to meet her green eyes anymore. Green like algae, or sea glass. Like a memory off in the distance she couldn't reach. She shook herself. "Let's get you into some warm clothes before you catch a chill again."

"Yeah. Okay."

## Chapter Eleven

*A*lora hated what they were going to have to do. She understood it. She knew they couldn't just leave the creature in the lake to drown people and terrorize and wreak havoc. She knew she needed its heart. But she couldn't shake what Eos had said. That the creature was probably hurting. That it didn't do the things it was doing by choice. It did them out of some warped necessity. Like breathing or eating. That it was just like Eos.

"Why do I have to stay here?" Declan whined, his galoshes smacking against the muddy bank.

"Everyone is staying here," Basanti said with a roll of her eyes. "Which I don't agree with. For the record."

"Not everyone. Arty's going." Bimala was bent behind a tripod, setting it up so they could get footage of the lake. Alora wasn't sure what for; they weren't planning to use this in their web-series, but Bimala always seemed to want to document everything. The researcher in her, Alora guessed.

"I should be going." Eos looked positively livid with this turn of events. "I'm the one who can communicate with it."

"You're the only one who's *tried* to communicate with it," Arty pointed out and took a step onto the dock. Eos glared at her, black eyes narrowed to slits.

"You're not going. And that's final." Alora stood up straighter, her hand tight around the strap of the duffle over her shoulder.

"You're not my master," Eos snapped, her mouth twitching with anger.

"No. I'm not. But that thing out there wanted you to join it, and you couldn't fight it off. So, you're not going, and that's all there is to it." Alora didn't wait for Eos to argue further. She spun on her heel and headed down the dock to climb into the boat beside Arty. The truth of it was that she didn't think she'd be able to handle it if something happened to Eos on her watch. Not now that . . . She shook herself; she'd worry about that later.

"She'll be all right," Arty said, seeming to read her thoughts.

"I'm not worried about her." But it sounded like a lie even to Alora. She tugged at the turtleneck that clung to her neck. She'd found it at one of the little stores in town, and the neck was too tight. But she didn't want her team to see the mark and how it had spread. She knew eventually she'd have to come clean about it. She'd have to show them what she was becoming, although even she wasn't sure what it was. But she hoped she could lift the curse before they ever had to know.

"Do you have a plan of how you're going to subdue the creature?"

No one had asked her that yet. They'd all just assumed she had a plan, like always. Alora was grateful for that. She didn't want to have to tell them she was just winging it. She didn't want them to find out that what she was about to do would probably cost her more of herself. In some distant place she felt fear about the choice she'd made. But it was so far away, and everything else was calm, cold determination that it felt like it belonged to someone else entirely. She knew what she was doing, and she knew it would work.

"You're going to use your magic." Arty didn't even question it. She also didn't sound particularly surprised. "You know what that will cost you."

"I don't see where I have much choice."

The boat sputtered across the water. The moon high in the sky. There had been no shift in the surface yet, no trace of the creature that lurked in the depths of the lake. Alora wondered if she'd have to use its name to force it out of hiding.

"Do you know how much time something like that will shave off from what she gave you?" Arty asked, sounding like there was something else she wanted to say. A warning she wanted to give, but she didn't.

"No." Alora didn't know, and she was trying not to think about it. She had little doubt after the events of the night prior that six months wasn't even close to the amount of time she had left anymore. "I don't want to know."

"You could use a weapon. You could borrow a spear gun from the town or get a rifle. That's what other hunters would do." Arty's words had an edge to them. Sharp, and cutting. But Alora knew she wasn't the one Arty was angry with. That it was the other humans who would do such a thing. The others who would use weapons against a creature without fully understanding it. Alora was different. Or, at least, she hoped so.

"Eos says it's in pain. I want to put it out of its misery, not cause it more hurt." She killed the engine, ignoring the way the last ripples of sound echoed off the water toward the shore. This far out, her team were tiny dots on the horizon, each of them dressed in dark clothes so they wouldn't draw attention, a little smear against the lights from the inn. They wouldn't be able to help her if she needed it. It was just her and Arty.

Arty made a noise, like a grunt of acknowledgment, or perhaps it was of amusement—it was hard to tell. Then she moved to the rail of the boat and leaned over the edge to look down into the inky depths.

"How long ago did you turn into . . . whatever you are?" Alora asked, hoping to keep the silence at bay a little bit longer. She didn't like it. It was charged, and creeping. Like waiting for the sound of thunder after a lightning strike and holding your breath. One—one thousand. Two—one thousand. Three—one thousand.

"I didn't turn into whatever I am." Arty snorted. She dipped over the rail to brush her fingers against the surface of the water, all pretense of being a frail old woman gone. "I, like your mermaid, was born what I am. And gave it up to be with a human."

"She's not with me," Alora said, the words hollow in her chest. They should hurt more, she recognized. They should squeeze her insides. For she had grown to like Eos in a way that was maybe not strictly platonic. But all they did was echo. Like the thing that would be hurt by them wasn't there anymore. "And she's going back to where she came from when all this is over."

"Is that what you really want?"

It wasn't. They both knew that. But Alora wasn't going to give the old bat the satisfaction of saying it out loud. Instead, she moved to the bow of the boat and leaned over it to glare at the smooth water. "What's taking it so long?"

"Maybe it had its fill with your little fish friend. She is magic, after all."

"But I saved her."

"Doesn't mean it didn't take something from her." Arty shrugged and moved to lean against the helm, her arms crossed.

"You're absolutely no help. Why did I even bring you?"

"I don't know. Why *did* you bring me?"

Alora couldn't tell if Arty was trying to get a rise out of her or if she was genuinely curious, and, to be frank, she didn't have time for her nonsense. She reached into the bag she'd brought along and pulled the book from it. Using her phone as a light, she flipped to the dog-eared page. The words were in Gaelic, which wasn't one of the languages she'd ever bothered to learn, but some Google translating and a couple hours of practice had provided her with what she needed.

She whispered the creature's name into the air, letting it drift across the still night like a leaf on water. Nothing happened. She huffed and said it again, a little louder, letting it carry.

"You're not doing it right." Arty scoffed.

"You said names have power. This should work." Alora snapped the book shut so she could glare at the darkened figure of Arty.

"It would if you meant it."

"Meant it?" Alora stood, rocking back on her heels.

"You're just saying the words. You aren't putting any feeling behind them. You have to mean it when you use words that way. Like you did when you ordered Eos to breathe. You meant it. That's the only way the magic will work."

"I do mean it."

"Do you? Or are you afraid it's going to hurt again?" Arty tilted her head like a bird, her eyes sharp and reflecting the light of Alora's phone.

Damn it. She was right. Alora was afraid it would hurt again. She knew it was going to. It was going to burn, just like it did before. That's why she'd worn so many layers. That's why there was an extra blanket stuffed into her bag. She tugged at the turtleneck, which suddenly felt like it was choking her.

"Try again."

Alora grumbled a little but opened the book again. She took a breath and forced the words from her lips, loud and commanding. They formed like letters in the air, rippling with light as they drifted across the water and then sank down into its depths to call the creature forward.

And then she heard it: the soft lap of water on the side of the boat, rocking it gently as the head of the creature came into view. With eyes all pupil, it was hard to tell where the creature was focused, but Alora felt it was assessing her.

"Now what?" Arty asked.

"Now, we get it on board the boat."

"Alora, it's not going to fit."

"Then what would you suggest?"

The creature crept closer, its hand lifting from the water to reach for Alora. She thought for a moment that maybe she'd have time to convince it to follow them to shore. Maybe she'd have the chance to escape. But no. Its hand flew out at her, grabbing her by the waist and pulling her into the water with it. She thought she heard Eos scream before she was pulled under.

She had just enough time to suck in a breath, and then she was pulled into the murky depths. It was too dark to see anything, but she knew it was pulling her to the bottom. She lashed out at the creature, catching it in what felt like one of its enormous eyes hard enough to make it loosen its grip. Alora kicked to the surface, taking a moment to suck in a breath.

The creature followed right behind her, its head peeking out, and Alora did the only thing she could think to do.

"Sleep! Be at peace," she ordered, and it didn't even take a full count to ten before the creature was floating on its back in the water. Grabbing one of its skeletal wrists, she dragged it back toward the boat. Alora coughed up water as she latched onto the rail. "Get me the rope."

Arty was already waiting with it, her hands steady. "Are you ready for what comes next?"

"Do I have a choice?"

"It won't wake now that you've told it to sleep. It'll go in peace."

"Yeah. That makes me feel better." Alora snorted, holding her hand out for the knife she'd stuffed into the duffle along with everything else. It *did* make her feel better, but only a little. She didn't like the idea of killing something, even something that had hurt people. Not like this. "Get the jar ready."

"Aye aye, captain."

Alora forced herself not to gag, swallowing bile, as she cut into the creature's narrow chest. It didn't so much as squirm against the pain, too deeply asleep to even notice. Alora wasn't sure how that had worked, but she decided it didn't matter. Distantly, she remembered peeling back the creature's skin and reaching beneath its rib cage to pull out the still-beating heart. But something cold had washed over her. Whatever human part of herself might have been revolted by it and sobbed — that part was dormant.

Alora hardly even blinked when the heart landed in the jar with a wet thud.

"We should get back." Arty had pulled the extra blanket from the duffle, ready to help wrap it around Alora. But Alora shrugged her off.

"I'm fine. Let's just go." Alora watched for a moment as

the creature sank back down to the depths where it had come from. She wondered, as the engine grumbled to life, why the creature had been in pain. What it had sacrificed to wind up where it was. If it had loved. Alora shook off those thoughts and maneuvered the boat back around, heading toward shore.

## Chapter Twelve

"It's kind of gross looking, isn't it?" Basanti asked, tapping her fingernail against the glass of the heart's jar. Her dark eyes were narrowed in suspicion.

"Oh, it's totally gross," Bimala agreed, but she was still smiling just a little, her eyes alight with a curiosity that Eos didn't really understand. Couldn't these humans just . . . leave well enough alone?

"Stop poking at it!" Alora snapped, scooping up the jar and tucking it back into her satchel. Her green eyes were hard. "It's not a toy, and it's not a science experiment."

And as Eos watched her, she had to wonder how the others hadn't noticed the change in Alora. They didn't seem bothered at all by the darkness that had crept up along her jaw to swallow up the freckles on her left cheek. Or how the woman in white's mark twisted and writhed like eels down near her wrist, just peeking out from under her sleeve. Or the hard set to her lips, anger simmering just below the surface that Eos hadn't seen there before. How long would it be before whatever it was took over completely? Before there was nothing of Alora left to save?

Eos shook herself. It wasn't her place to worry about such things.

"What's next?" Emrys, the only smart one out of the lot, asked. He'd positioned himself as far as he could from the still-beating thing and refused to even look at it. As if making eye contact with it would hurt him somehow. Or perhaps he just didn't have the stomach for blood, as so many humans didn't.

"Next, we find the woman in white." Arty's fingers drummed against an old leather-bound book she'd pulled from somewhere in her suitcase. Eos wondered how much of her library she'd packed with her. There seemed to be a never-ending supply of texts, and the humans had somehow failed to notice that as well.

"So we're going back to Dent?" Declan cocked his head.

"I think that's where we're going to have to start," Bimala said over the screen of the computer, her fingers making soft clacking sounds on the keyboard. "Although it doesn't look like she stayed there after we left. Which is lucky since we didn't exactly solve that problem in our rush to help Alora."

"We didn't have time to waste." Basanti huffed.

"I'm not saying we did."

"Moving on," Alora said, her back hitting the wall where she leaned, the heart of the creature tucked safely to her chest in her satchel. Her arms had curled around it as if she could keep anyone else from so much as looking at it. "Since she's not there anymore, we have the chance to hunt her down ourselves. Maybe giving us the element of surprise."

"Why do we need the element of surprise? We aren't going to attack her." Declan fidgeted, shifting his weight from one side to the other in his chair.

No one said anything and Declan's fidgeting got worse, the chair under him creaking with it.

"We aren't going to attack her, right?"

"We might have to." Arty shrugged. "Besides, it'll be good for her to feel like she's cornered if we want her to take this exchange. Maybe it'll make her careless, and she won't notice that this isn't actually the Witch of the Deep's heart."

"What happened to the equivalent exchange?" Emrys frowned.

"Just because it has the same amount of power, and is also a sea creature, doesn't mean she won't sense the difference. Especially if she's met Eos before."

"Especially with me right there," Eos mumbled.

"And she did ask for Eos specifically," Arty continued, as if Eos hadn't spoken at all.

"Who said you're going to be right there?" Alora's head jerked, her eyes narrowing on Eos, and Eos frowned.

"I did." Eos shrugged, unbothered by the intense stare as she met Alora's gaze.

"Well, you're not. It's too dangerous," Alora growled.

"I didn't exactly ask for permission."

"So?"

Eos tilted her chin back, refusing to give in. She could feel an argument coming, but she wasn't going to let Alora run off and face the woman in white by herself again. Not after what happened last time. Not if she could help her.

"Eos."

"Alora."

"As charming as this is, and it is, I could cut the tension with a knife," Arty said, and Eos ripped her eyes away from Alora to glare at Arty. "The fact of the matter is, we need all the help we can get. And although I know Eos doesn't have access to her powers right now, in the event that she really needs them, she might. So. Let's just agree that everyone is going."

"It's a stupid idea," Alora muttered.

Arty didn't look at all perturbed by being called stupid.

"Won't she try to get to Eos when she realizes who she is?" Declan had leaned forward to brace himself on his knees. He was the only one of the humans, other than Alora, who seemed truly concerned by what might happen to her. And Eos appreciated the gesture.

"We'll put her in a wig," Basanti said, unbothered.

*A wig*, Eos thought with some irritation, but she didn't glare daggers at Basanti. Or rather, she didn't have to as Alora was already doing that quite nicely.

"Bimala, where should we start?" Arty turned to Bimala, who was still tapping away at her computer, seeming to decide the discussion was closed. But Eos knew it wasn't. Eos and Alora would be talking about it more when there were fewer ears in the room, and she had little doubt that she'd be getting an earful of all the things Alora disliked about this plan. Not that it mattered; there wasn't really a better one. And Eos wasn't going to tell her that she knew being there might save Alora. In the end, if Arty's idea didn't work . . . She shook herself. She'd cross that bridge when she came to it.

"They've had several attacks on people out in the country that fit our parameters. We'll start there after we check on Dent to make sure she's not just dormant."

"Very specific." Alora's tone was annoyed, but she had the good grace to say it quietly.

"Actually, it is." Bimala narrowed her eyes on Alora, not bothering to cover her displeasure. "I have us booked for a train to the last town in two days. That'll give us time to check out Dent and be on our way. Hopefully we can track her from there."

"Any ideas how we're going to do that exactly?" Emrys moved away from the wall, stepping over to peer at Bimala's screen from behind her. "Track her, that is."

"Not really." Bimala frowned down at the screen, her shoulders hunching forward.

"Scrying." Arty shrugged, dropping the book she'd been looking at onto the coffee table in the center of the room. It thunked, the sound seeming to echo in Eos's ears. "She cursed Alora, in Dent, right? And that's where you think her home is. Stands to reason that we should be able to find something of hers there strong enough to help us along. Hair would do fine."

"Scry? Like . . . witches?" All the color had washed from Declan's face.

"Witches aren't the only ones who use scrying, kid. But yeah, like witches."

Eos didn't lean over to look at the book. She didn't care enough, she told herself, to even bother with it. But the humans all rose to cluster around it. All except Alora, who was still curled around the heart, her fingers twitching.

"Scrying will only give us a current location." Eos crossed her arms over her chest to keep herself where she was, away from Alora and that infernal organ, narrowing her eyes on Arty. "It won't allow us to follow her."

"It won't," Arty agreed all too readily. "But I figure once we're in range, Alora should be able to sense her. Like calling to like and all that."

"Alora isn't *like* her," Eos hissed, her fingers tightening into fists where they were tucked behind her arms.

Arty raised a brow as if to ask, *Isn't she?* But she let the question hang between them instead of voicing it. Eos didn't see Alora tense, but she could feel the way the temperature dropped with her tension. Neither monster turned their eyes to Alora, even as they sensed the danger.

"Either way," Arty said, finally, dispelling some of the heaviness in the air. "The woman in white will have left a piece of herself in Alora when she cursed her. All Alora need do is tell that piece to help her find its maker. Easy peasy."

"So, use her magic." Eos's tone had gone deceptively flat, hiding the anger that coiled like a sea serpent in her gut. Eos's eyes flicked around the room, looking at the others' faces, begging for one of the humans to agree with her. For them to see how dangerous this was. But they all looked to Alora instead. "And potentially speed up her change."

"Which won't matter, so long as we get the woman in white to accept the heart and remove the curse," Alora said, her voice oddly calm for someone who was gambling her humanity on something that had a very small chance of working. "That's what we'll do then." Alora pushed off from the wall. "In the meantime, we should all get some rest. The train leaves early tomorrow."

## Chapter Thirteen

*S*ummer was well and truly on its way, Alora knew that. She knew that even the nights had heated up to be comfortable for the others in her group. But still she felt the chill of it seep into her skin. She'd bought a few more turtlenecks before leaving Scotland, tugging them up to her chin, even on days when the others were in tank tops.

No one seemed to notice how she hid her slightly purple lips under a thick layer of lipstick, the cold that seemed to numb her fingertips constantly, or the way she huddled into the corner of the train with her sleeves pulled down over her hands. No one except Eos, whose gaze lingered constantly on Alora.

Alora wondered if maybe the humans couldn't see the mark. Maybe they didn't see how it had spread. Maybe it was just her and the monsters now. Or rather . . . just the monsters. Since she was becoming one herself.

Sometime over the next few days as they traveled to Dent, Alora stopped in front of a mirror while in the restroom. It was then that she noticed the change in her eyes. Their usually warm green, the color of lush under-growth, was turning colder. Like frozen, dead things.

"It's gotten worse," Eos had said when she'd caught Alora looking at the mark in the mirror of the train bath-room. She'd tugged the collar of her turtleneck down enough that she could see the way the woman in white's fingers clutched at her throat, nearly covering it entirely in mottled, flaking skin. "Even if we do get her to remove it, it's probably going to scar."

"Are you even a proper monster hunter if you haven't gotten cursed a time or two?" she'd asked with a shrug, her voice deceptively light. But Eos was right; she'd never be the same after this was all said and done. Even if Arty's plan did work. And Alora was . . . Well, Alora was terrified.

That's why she didn't even blink as Bimala pointed out the woman in white's house and they planned to go in and retrieve whatever they could to help with the scrying. It would just be her and Emrys, with the twins acting as lookout and Arty and Declan poised to run interference. They'd left Eos at the hotel, in spite of her glaring, because Alora needed her away from all of this. She needed her *safe*.

"I feel like breaking and entering the house of a creature who has cursed you, may I add, is a very bad idea," Emrys said, his flashlight glaring in Alora's eyes. She hissed and knocked it away.

"It's not breaking. We have a key." She held it up to show him one more time before jamming it into the lock and jiggling it until the door unlatched.

"Which we got from the neighbor under false pretenses. So kind of the same thing." Emrys nudged the door shut slowly behind them, casting his light on the floor. "Besides, how do we even know for sure that this is the woman in white? Bimala has been wrong before."

"It's her," Alora said with such certainty that she felt it

down to her very marrow. The air in the house was thick with something—resentment, maybe. Alora felt like she was wading through Jell-O just trying to walk across the living room.

"What if she's here?" Emrys asked, his voice almost soft enough to hide the quiver of fear. Almost. Alora heard it even still. She couldn't tell if becoming a monster had made her more attuned to the fear of mortals or if she just knew him that well.

"She's not." The stairs creaked under their weight, making Emrys's breaths come a little shallower, a little more panicked. But Alora didn't stop and wait for him to follow. She walked on, somehow able to make out the layout of the place even in the dark. Her heart leapt a little at the realization, but Alora forced herself to breathe through it.

Down the hall, to the last door on the right—her bedroom. Alora could feel it. This was where she'd . . . Where she'd become whatever she'd become.

"How do you—"

"Because I *know*, Emrys. Now shut up and help me find a hairbrush," Alora snapped, moving over to the nightstand to dig through the drawer in search of a brush, or a hair tie with some hairs stuck to it, or something, anything. This place was giving her a headache, she couldn't explain it. There was something . . . lingering in the air. Something she couldn't quite hear, but that seemed to be ringing in her ears even still. Like pressure building there first and then spreading to her temples.

"I've got something," Emrys said after what felt like forever.

Alora turned from where she'd been digging around in the woman's vanity to see Emrys holding a bright-orange brush in his hand. "Are there any hairs in it?"

"Several. So we should be good."

"Let's get out of here."

As soon as they were out in the cool night air again, Alora felt the pressure abate. Like a weight lifting off her entire body. She let out a long, low breath, her shoulders hunching forward.

"Hey. Are you all right?" Emrys reached for her, and she jerked back, not wanting him to feel how cold her skin was. If she could keep them from noticing a little longer, it'd be over soon. All of it.

"I'm fine." She tucked the key back into her pocket and turned to walk back down the street the way they'd come.

"Are you sure? You don't . . . You haven't been yourself lately, Alora."

"I said I'm *fine*, Emrys." Alora's teeth ground together, and she drew in a long breath to calm herself. It wouldn't do to yell at him. It would prove that something was wrong.

"You don't seem fine," Emrys mumbled.

"Well I—"

The woman in white. Standing there in the middle of the street. Her arms limp at her sides. Skin ghostly white, only made lighter by the dark hair that hung lank over her shoulders, washed silver in the moonlight. Her head tilted at an angle that was entirely unnatural while a streetlight over top of her flickered.

"Emrys, when I tell you, you need to run," Alora said, keeping her tone carefully neutral as she tried to breathe through the rush of fear flooding her lungs.

"What? Why?" She could hear the frown in his voice, but she wasn't going to turn around to see it. Because she wasn't going to take her eyes off the creature at the end of the lane.

"Just do as I say."

Emrys couldn't see *her*. If he could, he would be panicking more, Alora knew that. Which meant that she was more of a danger to him now than ever. And Alora was not about to risk anyone else. Not when she could save him.

For a moment they stayed still, their breaths puffing in the air as the temperature dropped steadily. Then the woman in white opened her mouth, black teeth glistening in the light, and a loud screech rent the air. Emrys might not be able to see her, but he heard her. He jolted beside Alora.

"Alora, what the hell was—"

"Sh."

The woman in white lifted an arm, and suddenly she was right in front of Alora, her cold fingertips gripping Alora by the jaw.

"Run," Alora said with all the urgency of someone who knew what would happen if the woman in white touched him. "Get out of here. Now!"

And Emrys, Amphitrite bless him, took off like a bat out of hell, his sneakers slapping against the uneven pavement.

"You have returned," the woman in white said, her grip loose around Alora's throat. Just enough that she could feel the cold seeping into her skin through the fabric of her turtleneck. "Have you brought me what I have asked for?"

Alora opened her mouth to tell the woman in white that she did have it, but it just wasn't there with her right in that moment. The woman in white tightened her hold, stilling Alora's words in her throat.

"Do not lie."

Alora swallowed, the sound loud in her ears, and tried to push the words past her tongue. But they wouldn't budge. Instead, what came out was, "I can't give you the Witch of the Deep's heart. But I have another. One that's just as powerful. You can have that one."

"You what?" the woman in white hissed, her nails digging into the mottled skin of Alora's throat, pinpricks of pain that made Alora's eyes burn with tears.

"I brought another heart. A creature from a lake in Scotland. It killed — "

"It won't work."

"Why not?" Alora kept her hands at her sides by force, even as they itched to pry the cold fingers from her neck. She could feel the mark squirming under her skin again. Feel it spreading, burning cold through her veins, making her skin raise in goosebumps and her teeth chatter. What would happen when it reached her eyes?

"Because I can't just take it. In order for it to retain its magic, the heart has to be given to me by the person themselves or their soulmate. Willingly."

"Soul . . . soulmate?" Alora frowned, confusion coloring the words. Soulmate. That . . . Didn't fit. Did it?

"The heart you brought, of that creature?" the woman in white continued as if Alora hadn't spoken. "It doesn't retain any of its magic. It is a dead thing."

"It still beats."

"It is a dead thing."

"Soulmates?" Alora couldn't get away from that word. It bounced off the inside of her mind like a ping pong ball. Soulmates. Grandma Roan had always talked about them. About how the people of the sea didn't just believe in them, but saw them as a fact of life.

"You have a week. Bring me the heart of the Witch of the Deep."

"And if I don't?" Alora lifted her chin, her eyes narrowing.

"You know what will happen." The woman in white shrugged. And then she disappeared. The grip she'd had on Alora's throat now gone, Alora slumped forward, clawing at the turtleneck. She gasped for breath, sucking down the cold air in spite of how it burned at her throat. Then, when she had recovered, she straightened her clothes, pulled her collar back into place, and started at a measured pace back toward the hotel.

They were waiting for her in the lobby. Her team. They looked like they had been about to head out to get her.

"Alora," Eos breathed, her hands twitching at her sides as if she might reach for Alora, but she didn't, and for once Alora was grateful for it. She needed space to understand all that was between herself and Eos. To understand what it meant to be someone's soulmate, and if it had anything at all to do with that strange warmth she'd felt in her chest for weeks now.

Instead, it was Basanti at her side suddenly, her hands taking Alora's cold fingers in between her own. "Are you all right? What happened?"

"I'm going to kill her. I'm going to kill the woman in white," Alora declared, tearing her hand from Basanti's. "Find me a way to do that."

"Aye aye, captain." Arty gave a little salute.

"Alora?" Basanti asked, her eyes huge and a little glassy.

"I'm fine. Now, find me a way to kill a ghost."

## Chapter Fourteen

"There's a dagger," Arty whispered into the night like a secret, like a promise of danger, like a lie.

The others had gone to bed long ago, leaving just Arty, Alora, and Eos in the tiny study at the bed-and-breakfast where they had taken up residence. Just them. The three monsters. The ones who didn't even need sleep anymore, as far as Eos knew.

But Arty and Alora seemed to have forgotten she was there, their backs to her as they bent over more thick leather-bound books from Arty's suitcase.

"What kind of dagger?" Alora asked, her voice a hush in the silence of the room. There was a tremor of hope in her words, like what Arty was offering was too good to be true, and in Eos's opinion it probably was. Arty had proven useful, but Eos still wasn't sure that she trusted the old monster. Not when Arty wouldn't reveal what she really was. Not when the creature hid behind the mask of a feeble old lady. Everyone had their own motivations, and Arty was no different.

"The kind that can kill a ghost." Arty's eyes were sharp,

hungry. Even with her face only visible in profile, Eos could see it. She hoped Alora could see it too.

But Alora didn't even flinch at the expression. She simply nodded. "Where will we find it?"

"Oh, child, no." Arty laughed, the sound soft and condescending. Eos fought the urge to rip the book from her hands and shoo her away. To chase her back to that creaking house on the hill. That's where they should have left her, where they found her. She'd been nothing but trouble since. "We'll have to forge it ourselves. But first we'll have to retrieve ore from an underground cave off the coast, near where you found the Witch of the Deep."

"You know how to forge such a blade?" Eos asked, drawing their attention to her for the first time in well over an hour.

"I've done it before," Arty said, looking at her like she was not at all surprised Eos was still there. Like maybe she'd sensed her the entire time. She probably had. Alora was still getting used to the way a monster's senses could reach out beyond a human's, but Arty had had decades, perhaps centuries, of practice with them. "When my wife and I . . ." Arty cleared her throat, shaking her head. Her eyes had filled with something—sadness maybe—the first real emotion that Eos thought she may have seen from the old monster before it was gone. "Anyway. Yes. I've done it before. I can do it again. We just need the ore."

"It'll be dangerous to go diving there." Eos moved over to them, leaning on the back of Alora's chair to eye Arty, suspicion in her gaze. What was the old monster getting out of this? "The creatures of the deep don't take kindly to intruders. Least of all humans."

"Well, it's a good thing we have the Witch of the Deep with us then. Isn't it?" Arty smiled, the expression not reaching her eyes, and Eos felt a chill roll down her spine.

·≬≬·

A FEW HOURS LATER, Eos was strapped with a diving tank and some fake flippers, sitting on the edge of a boat. She'd made the decision to go with Alora. She couldn't let Alora go alone, not down there, not when she might be able to help. And she felt a not-so-subtle trepidation from all the others. So it would just be them. Them and their fake flippers, and a soft crackle of a radio in her ear.

Under the water it was almost like being home again. Almost like returning to the place where she'd come from. Only . . . not at all the same. Because she realized, the deeper they dove, this place no longer belonged to her.

The deep didn't belong to her, and she didn't belong to it. And all around her was silence. No soft whisper in the dark of a squid passing. No fluttering minds of a school of jelly. Just silence. Maybe it was true what she'd heard humans say: you couldn't ever go home, not how it was, not how you were, not really.

Eos felt that. With a new name, and a new life, and a new . . . whatever Alora was to her, she did not belong to the deep anymore. It was sad, but Eos didn't feel that sadness as deeply as she might have weeks ago.

"This way." Alora's voice crackled in the speaker in her ear, breaking Eos from her thoughts.

Eos nodded and turned to follow her. The gear they were wearing weighed her down, but she pushed forward. She had been made for swimming, once. It didn't feel like that anymore.

Alora switched on a light as they approached the mouth of a cave. The darkness yawned before them like the jaws of a beast, and Eos had to stop herself from reaching out to grab Alora's wrist. They were so close now. So very close. She couldn't rip this away from Alora. She couldn't take away the chance that Alora could be human, normal, again.

The beam of the flashlight was eaten up by the darkness, showing only a small circle of whatever lay in front of them. But Eos knew what they were looking for. She could feel the hum of the magic in the stone around them.

In the dark, Eos could also feel something watching them. Its gaze heavy on the back of her neck as she swam to the cave wall, putting her hand against it. It was warm to the touch, strange when they'd already gone so deep. So deep.

"Alora, we need to hurry up." Eos's eyes swept through the dark around them. Searching for the gleam of light reflected on a black eye. Searching for some sign that they were not safe. Some excuse for the paranoia crawling up from the base of her spine.

"Just a minute." Alora pulled a little pickaxe from her belt and got to work chipping away at the wall. The sound was oddly muffled in the water.

Something shifted in the dark, though Eos wasn't sure how she knew. For without her powers, it was hard to see the difference in the black that would differentiate a cave wall and a living thing. Hard to know what was watching and waiting. But there could be any number of things hiding out in a cave. Any number of predators. A squid. A shark. A giant eel. And things even she didn't have a name for. Things that writhed with the shadows and snuffed out the light. Things she had used to down ships and drown humans. Things she had fed and helped to make strong.

"Alora . . ." Eos reached for her magic, hoping that with the weight of the sea pressing in on her, maybe it would answer her. Maybe it would at least give her enough to be able to reach out her senses and speak to the creature. To tell it not to attack. No luck. There was a cold, empty space where her magic used to be. Like someone had reached into her and carved it out of her. It left Eos aching.

"Almost there, almost there." Eos could see Alora wearing on her lower lip through the clear plastic of the face mask, her concentration fixated solely on getting the chunk of rock free from the wall.

Eos turned so her back was to Alora, her eyes swiveling around them through the dark. She really should have brought her own light. She should have taken Basanti's advice.

Something brushed Eos's leg.

The creature in the dark twisted its tentacle around Eos's ankle. Her breath came in hard pants, fogging up the plastic of her mask. At the same moment, she heard Alora muttering a triumphant, "Got it."

"Good, let's go." Eos jerked her ankle, trying to get free of the creature, but it tightened its grip, pain lancing up her leg as it nearly crushed the bone. She felt the color wash from her face.

"Eos?" Alora asked, turning to look at her with wide eyes. "What's wrong?"

"She's here." Eos didn't know how she knew. She'd never even seen the woman in white. And she was pretty sure the woman in white didn't have tentacles. But no . . . that wasn't a tentacle, was it? When she looked down, the light from Alora's flashlight caught on the bone-white glow of fingers wrapped around her ankle, with too many joints.

And then the hand gave a hard yank, trying to tug Eos down, down into the depths. Deeper than she ever remembered having gone.

"Oh no you don't," Alora growled, grabbing her by the waist and kicking at the arm. The heel of her flipper connected with the creature's wrist. "Let her go."

*We had a deal. This one is mine. You brought her to me!*

The words twisted like a serpent through the water, winding their way around Eos's body. Tightening around her lungs. And then she felt it—a break in her line. The air she needed to breathe turned into so many bubbles.

"Enough!" Alora shouted, lacing her words with the power that simmered under her skin. "Let her go!"

The hand jerked away as if burned. And for a moment Eos wondered if the woman in white had even really been there at all, as she had disappeared entirely. Or maybe that was the lack of oxygen talking.

Alora looped her arms tight around Eos's waist and kicked off. She dragged Eos back through the cave. Eos kicked her flippers, trying to help as much as she could, but the darkness was closing in now. Her vision narrowed to a point. And the last thing she thought before she lost consciousness was that the humans were right, after all.

She couldn't go home. She'd never be able to go home. She'd have to find a new home. Or make one. Or something. Because she didn't belong in the sea anymore, and she never would again. Even if she got her tail back.

THERE WAS warmth around her when she came to, a fluffy blanket pulled up to her chin, and soft murmuring of conversation. And she was alive, Eos realized with no small amount of wonder. The humans had pulled her from the water and seen to her care. Even when they didn't have to. Even when she wasn't one of them.

"She's awake," Declan whispered, and his tone sounded excited as he moved to kneel beside the couch where they laid her. His blue eyes were wide and soft with concern. "How're you feeling?"

"You had us worried there for a minute." Bimala held

out a cup of water as Declan reached to help Eos sit up, his hands gentle.

"You've been out a couple of days. Alora's climbing up the damn walls." Basanti rolled her eyes.

"Are you hungry?" Emrys asked. "We've got soup in the kitchen; I can heat some up."

"Stop hovering over her. Let the girl breathe for a minute. She nearly suffocated after all." Basanti scoffed, her tone annoyed, but she didn't look annoyed. She looked . . . oh Amphitrite, she looked worried. They all looked so worried. Why were they worried about her? She wasn't one of them. She wasn't—Oh.

Oh.

Maybe she was one of them. This must be what it was like to have a family.

"I'm all right, thank you," Eos whispered, her voice scratchy with disuse. "Where's Alora?"

"Out in the shed working on that damn dagger. Arty dragged her out there. Said if she didn't keep her hands busy, she'd lose her mind. She was probably right." Basanti shrugged.

"So we got the ore."

"Yes. And when Alora came back up, she looked . . ." Declan let out a breath, shaking his head, his face set in an expression he usually reserved for the monsters they hunted.

"Looked how?"

"Let's just say, I'd hate to be the woman in white."

"She said the woman in white was down there with you?" Bimala asked, her tone curious again, eyes bright behind her spectacles.

"I don't know if it was her exactly." Eos sighed, handing over her cup of water so Declan could set it on the coffee table. "Maybe it was just the fear, or the enclosed space, or something. Or maybe it was something else . . . one of the ghosts of someone I killed before Alora brought me to the surface." She shrugged, not really interested in knowing the answer. She didn't see why it mattered. "Whatever it was, it tried to keep me there. And Alora didn't let it."

"Well," Bimala said, pushing her glasses up her nose, and it felt like the closing of a subject. Eos desperately wanted to hug her for that, but she didn't. "It's over now. You should eat something. It'll be our turn to hunt her soon."

## Chapter Fifteen

*T*he dagger burned Alora wherever it touched her. So much so she wondered how she'd even wield it against the woman in white. Maybe she was just . . . too much monster, these days. Maybe she was fighting a losing battle. The thought seemed to sink into her skin, resting against her bones, just like the curse mark. Just like how the leathery skin of whatever she was becoming hugged them.

She'd never actually missed her normal, boring life before. Going to the grocery. Calls from her mom to nag her about settling down. Late-night k-drama marathons that bled into sleepy mornings. She did now. She missed all of it now. And Alora realized, perhaps too late, that the adventure she'd been chasing all her life, that shot of adrenaline whenever she came face to face with a monster? Maybe it was always meant to be the one thing that did her in. Maybe it was always going to end this way. And now she wasn't just going to miss the past, she was going to miss the future too.

Alora tossed the dagger to her non-dominant hand, the

one not totally eaten up by the curse yet. The one that was still human.

She hissed when even that burned, leaving behind a singed bit of skin on her palm that she'd have to hide under stretched-out sleeves. The dagger clattered to the ground, and she reached for the heavyweight gloves she'd used to forge the damn thing to pick it up. Maybe Grandma Roan had a pair of gloves in her trunk that she could borrow.

"How's it going out here?" Arty asked, poking her head in through the door.

"Fine. It's going fine," Alora said perhaps a little too quickly. Arty raised an eyebrow. Crap, yeah, it had definitely been too quickly.

"I found these old riding gloves in a chest upstairs. You should try them out. They'll cover the mark on your hand."

A blur of brown leather was Alora's only warning as Arty tossed the gloves at her. She snatched them up, the fingers of her left hand rough against the soft leather. Or . . . what she assumed to be soft leather. It was hard to feel anything through the hardened skin of her fingertips on that hand. The curse having taken even that from her.

"Thanks. These'll work great."

"We're heading out soon. Bimala and Basanti were able to scry for the woman in white. It looks like we've got a bit of a drive ahead of us. So you should get washed up."

"Right. I'll be in in a minute." Alora waited until Arty had headed back to the house before she let out the soft sob that had lodged in her throat. This was it. This was what she had to look forward to. She dropped the dagger onto the table and stripped her right hand of the thick work glove.

The riding glove was cool under the sweaty fingertips of her right hand. It was soft, she could feel that now with her still-human hand. The leather around the palm well-worn from where Grandma Roan had clutched the wheel of the car. She wondered if Grandpa Jiro had taught her, or if it'd been Milo. She wondered if she'd ever get the chance to teach Eos.

Scoffing, Alora scrubbed at her eyes. "Don't be stupid," she told herself. "When this is all over, she's going home."

And that would be the end of that. Eos would return to the deep, and Alora would . . . Alora would likely go back to her life as it had been. And that would be . . . Well, it wouldn't be fine. But it would be all right. She could live with that.

Taking a deep breath, she pulled on the gloves and picked up the dagger experimentally. They would do. They may not be a permanent solution, but they would work long enough for her to get rid of the woman in white.

"I don't like this," Bimala said, her footsteps soft in the undergrowth. They had all decided to follow her, in spite of Alora's protests. "What if she tries to take *your* heart?"

Alora's gaze flicked to Eos, who was some feet ahead, her head ducked as she and Declan chatted. She wondered for a brief moment when they had become friends, and then cast the thought aside. It didn't matter.

"She can't take what I've already given away." The words slipped from Alora's lips, half a joke. But as soon as they were out in the thick forest air, she knew they were true. When it had happened, she didn't know. Funny how a thing like that could sneak up on someone.

"Alora . . . One, I don't think that's how that works." Bimala rolled her eyes, letting out an exasperated huff. "Two, you don't even know her. Not really."

"Doesn't seem to matter." Alora shrugged and strode

away from Bimala, taking the lead in their little group, her camping gear thudding against her spine. She didn't know how long they'd have to camp out before they found the woman in white, but she hoped it wouldn't be long.

THE WOMAN in white was waiting for them on the night they thought *they* had caught up to *her*—she even said as much. Her lips curled back over black teeth like some kind of rabid animal, her eyes wild.

"You should have come alone," she said, the words a threat in the air. "You shouldn't have brought the witch with you."

She was right, Alora should have left them behind, especially Eos. She should have left all the humans safe at Grandma Roan's house where they wouldn't be in her way. Alora looked around and found the others frozen, their eyes unblinking, their mouths agape. Alora didn't know what the woman in white had done to them, but the only ones who were unaffected were herself and Arty. Arty, who had . . . who was . . . Arty. Where was Arty?

"The old monster ran away. It's just you and me now." The woman in white laughed, her steps slow and even as she advanced on Alora across the forest floor. Her strides were soundless on ground littered in dried leaves and tiny twigs. Her gaze flicked to Eos at Alora's side, her long gray hair rustling in the wind as she remained frozen. "You could do it now. No one would blame you if you did, not even her."

"Let them go." Alora gripped the dagger hard in her hand, the metal of the hilt digging in even through the leather gloves. She moved to stand between the woman in white and Eos. Not that she thought she could stop the woman in white from hurting Eos, but she could slow her down.

"Before it's too late," the woman in white continued as if Alora hadn't spoken. As if she wasn't holding a dagger that could end her existence. "I mean . . . already there are going to be side effects."

"Side effects?" The words ripped themselves from Alora's throat and her world tilted on its axis, her lungs struggling to draw adequate breath.

"Yes. There's no going back. You won't ever be human again, not really. But we can stop this here. We can keep you from changing any more than you already have. Maybe you could even go back to being . . . normal. Marry some nice human. Have children. Settle down. Isn't that what you want?"

"Why?" Alora had to know. She had to know why this was happening. Why she had been destined, or chosen, or just had the bad luck to receive this fate.

"Why what?"

"Why me?"

"I told you before," the woman in white said, and if her eyes weren't black as night without any definition for pupil or iris, Alora might have been able to see her rolling them. But as it stood, it was just a fluttering of lashes. "Because I couldn't have done it without you. You're the only one who can make her weak. Her soulmate."

The words echoed in the small clearing. Bouncing off trees and shrubs in the absence of birds and insects. And then the woman in white flickered, disappearing for a moment, only to reappear at Alora's side. Her hands outstretched for Eos. Alora didn't even think. She lunged. The dagger sliced through the air, aimed right for the woman in white's heart.

It plunged in, past the skin and the bone. But the

woman in white didn't stop. Her fingers wrapped around Eos's neck, pressing on her windpipe. Eos let out a sound like an injured animal, but she didn't move. She couldn't fight back. She couldn't breathe!

Alora twisted the dagger in the woman in white's chest, but the woman in white threw her head back and laughed. She stepped back, letting go of Eos, taking the dagger with her.

"Oh, you idiot girl. You aren't *human* anymore! You can't wield this thing!" She yanked it from her chest and dropped it to the forest floor without flinching. There wasn't even a tear left behind by the blade, no mark at all that Alora had buried it hilt deep in the woman in white's chest.

And then she lunged for Eos again. Her bone-white fingers reached into Eos's chest just as they had Alora's, and Alora did the only thing she could think to do.

She screamed.

She screamed like her heart might break if she stopped. She screamed like the noise alone would rip the thing from inside her that the woman in white had left behind. She screamed like her world was ending. Maybe it was.

Magic rushed from her in a wave of light so powerful it downed trees in its wake. It didn't touch Eos or her friends. But it threw the woman in white through the forest with such strength that Alora heard whatever unfortunate wood she finally stopped against crack under the force.

And then . . .

And then . .

And then .

She lost herself to the cold and the dark and the spread of the mark across her skin. She lost herself to the creature that had lived under the surface of her skin for Amphitrite knew how long.

Maybe it had always been there. Maybe it was the nightmares that lurked in the dark. Maybe it was the disquiet that came from staying in one place too long. Maybe it was the thing that snarled and wanted to lash out when her mother told her to give up chasing monsters and just be normal for once.

Maybe it had always been there.

Maybe it's who she really was.

## Chapter Sixteen

*H*er lips were blue, the warmth seeping out of her and into the magic that freed Eos and blew the woman in white away.

Her lips were blue.

Her eyelids stuck open, unblinking. The once–lush green irises washed of their color, turned gray and unseeing.

Her lips were blue. Her eyelids stuck open, unblinking.

Her fingers did not move. Did not tremble. Did not give any evidence that she was alive, much less awake. Not even a twitch.

Her lips were blue. Her eyelids stuck open, unblinking. Her fingers did not move.

And oh.

Oh gods.

Oh Amphitrite.

Oh no.

Her chest wasn't moving. She wasn't . . . she wasn't *breathing*, Eos realized perhaps too late, when the shock wore off.

*She's not breathing!*

Eos scrambled on her knees, reaching for Alora, pulling the other woman into herself. Her fingers tight on the fabric of Alora's jacket. The thick one. The one that was far *too* thick for the current weather. Seasonally inappropriate, Bimala had noted but hadn't asked about. Why hadn't she asked? Why hadn't they cared? Stupid humans! Couldn't they see?! Couldn't they see how Alora was hurting?! How she was wasting away.

A noise echoed off the emptiness of the clearing, the humans still frozen in their tracks, and it took Eos too long, *too long*, to realize that it was a sob ripped from her own throat. A wounded sound. The sound of someone who didn't have anything else to lose. How had she let it get this far? How had she not seen until it was too late?

Something snapped—a twig maybe. The sound of it was decisive, a message. Someone had stepped into the clearing, and Eos's head jerked up to meet the black gaze of the woman in white. She narrowed her eyes.

"Oh, little Witch of the Deep," the woman in white tsked, shaking her head. "I should kill you now. Take what is mine from you and her. Leave your bodies here for your friends to find."

"You can't hurt her!" Eos shifted, hunching herself over Alora's body, shielding her from the woman in white's cold gaze. She wouldn't. She couldn't. Let that woman do anything else. Take anything more from Alora.

"You underestimate me." The woman in white laughed.

Eos didn't care. She didn't. She saw the dagger where it had fallen, grabbed it up, and then, tucking Alora safely behind her, she rose from her knees. Putting herself in between the two.

"I'll hurt you," the woman in white warned. And suddenly she was in front of Eos, her grasp tight around

Eos's wrist. Keeping the dagger at bay while boney white fingers lifted to reach into Eos's chest and clutch at her lungs, restricting the air flow.

"You overestimate your abilities," Eos laughed, or tried to, but it was hard when there were spots swimming in front of her vision already. "You cannot hurt that which is already dead."

"You made me this." Her tone sounded accusing, her fingers tightening enough to make it so Eos couldn't even swallow past the burn of need for air. But that didn't matter. So long as she could keep the woman in white from hurting Alora and the others, it wouldn't matter. "You killed the man I loved."

"No," Eos said, the word grating in her throat as it forced itself past the woman in white's stranglehold. "*You* made you this." Her grip on the dagger tightened, but she didn't try to pull her wrist from the woman in white's hands. Not yet. "Becoming a monster is a choice that you make every single day. And I choose humanity. I choose mortality. If giving up magic means I get to really live again? If it means I get to make new memories? Then you can have it!"

And then she twisted her wrist away from the woman in white, pulling the dagger toward herself instead, and plunged it into her own chest. It hurt. Amphitrite it hurt. She hadn't been expecting it to hurt. Or . . . or maybe she had. She couldn't remember. She couldn't remember what her first death had felt like, the one where she'd sacrificed all that she was for a foolish girl in love. But . . . but death *hurt*.

And even if she thought she might survive it, she knew what the dagger would do. She didn't know how she knew. She just . . . she had picked it up and she'd understood. She may live on, but this would be a death of a kind. A loss of another piece of herself. Or perhaps just the final loss of the person she had been. The final thing the Witch of the Deep would give up so that Eos could live on.

"You . . . You're just . . ." The woman in white didn't seem to understand. Her eyes had gone wide and unfocused in her face as she watched the purple-and-black writhing magic wash from where the dagger had plunged into Eos's heart up her throat as the dagger me, and down her own arm. Into her own chest. Eos would be human after this. Human entirely. "You're just *giving* it to me?" The woman in white's words broke.

"You need to let go," Eos said, her free hand lifting to gently squeeze the woman in white's wrist. "Of the vengeance. Of your hate. Before it takes with it every happy memory you ever had with him. Before it takes with it who you are."

"Why?"

Eos's gaze flicked down to Alora. Her long red hair had spilled out at their feet like a tidal wave. Like a riptide threatening to pull them under. It was too late for that; Eos was already drowning in Alora, she realized. "I give you this, and you set her free. You give her back to me."

"No." The woman in white tried to pull her wrist from Eos's grasp. "No. I won't."

"You will." Eos tightened her grip, not letting the woman in white shake her loose. "Even if you don't want to. My magic has a will of its own, and it knows what to do. You will give her back to me. You will set us free. And I will never so much as see your shadow again. You will let this vengeance lie, and go off, and do something else with this magic."

"Or what?" the woman in white spat.

"The magic of the deep will eat you alive, just as it tried to eat me. It will leave you an aching hollow of what you once were. And in the end, you'll return to the deep, just as I did. And you'll spend your days making monsters, just as I did."

And then it was done. The magic had passed to the woman in white, the dagger had disintegrated into a fluttering of dust, and Eos slumped against her hold. Eos's magic, now singing under someone else's skin, did as it was bidden. It pulled the curse from Alora. It brought her back to herself. It freed the others. And then it sent the woman in white far, far, far away from them. To darken someone else's doorway.

Eos fell to her knees in the damp underbrush just in time for Alora to sit up and pull her in close. "She's gone," Eos said, pushing her face into Alora's shoulder and sucking in much needed air. "She's gone, and you're safe."

Alora didn't say anything. She held Eos tighter against her chest, and Eos realized that for the first time in her long, long life, she felt warm.

## Epilogue

"*A*re you packed and ready?" Alora asked from where she stood in the kitchen, finishing up clearing out the refrigerator. They didn't want to leave anything behind that would spoil in the month they'd be gone. Another job. Another monster.

"Yes. I'm just going to go down and give Amphitrite one final offering before we're off." Eos moved around the counter so she could press a kiss to Alora's cheek. "You should too. Make sure she remembers to look out for us."

"Like she'd forget." Alora scoffed, but she nodded. "I'll be down there in a minute. Just have to finish up here."

Alora leaned in to steal a real kiss, one from Eos's lips, as Eos stole an apple from the little bag Alora was packing for the plane and ducked out the back doors. Alora stood, watching her for a while as Eos kicked off her shoes haphazardly and started through the sand with a little smile on her face.

Then Alora looked down at her left hand, the dark lines of the woman in white's curse still etched into her skin like veins. They hadn't gone away when Eos had saved her.

They never would, Arty said when they'd finally caught up with her. But that didn't make her any less human. Didn't make her any more of a monster.

Because here was the thing about monsters. They were just people with magic who forgot who they were in the wake of pain and decided to make that everyone else's problem.

And while Alora had spent much of her life looking for a missing piece, the next bit of excitement, she didn't have to look anymore.

She'd found it.

# Acknowledgments

First off, thank you—the reader—for reading this continuation of Irsa's story. If you read the first book when it came out, I know you had a bit of a wait to get to Irsa's happy ending, and I really appreciate you hanging in there. I hope you'll drop a review on GoodReads to let me know what you think.

Next, I'd like the thank my small hoard of beta-readers. You guys gave some excellent insight, and I really appreciate all of your hard work. And my dear friend Tanya for giving this thing a critical eye.

And last but certainly not least, thank you to my writing community. Particularly, Tiss, Elle, and Jasmine who I have known for near a decade now—without you there would be no Lou. And to my new friends at MTP for being supportive and awesome.

## About the Author

Born and raised in a small town near the Chesapeake Bay, Lou Wilham grew up on a steady diet of fiction, arts and crafts, and Old Bay. After years of absorbing everything, there was to absorb of fiction, fantasy, and sci-fi she's left with a serious writing/drawing habit that just won't quit. These days, she spends much of her time writing, drawing, and chasing a very short Basset Hound named Sherlock.

When not, daydreaming up new characters to write and draw she can be found crocheting, making cute bookmarks, and marathoning whatever happens to catch her eye.

Learn more about Lou and her future projects on her website: http://louinprogress.com/ or join her mailing list at: http://subscribepage.com/mailermailer

facebook.com/LouWilham
instagram.com/lou.wilham

## More Books You'll Love

If you enjoyed this story,
please consider leaving a review.

Then check out more books from
Midnight Tide Publishing!

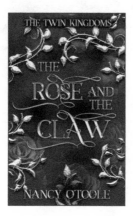

*The Rose and the Claw by Nancy O'Toole*

A woman on a mission...

Rose Gardner never thought she'd leave the small town of West Ridge. But when her husband dies at war, she must return his arms to his place of birth to set his spirit to rest. After traveling into enemy territory, Rose falls into a trap. Held captive in an enchanted manor, she finds herself face to face with a beast who is equally horrifying and kind. Will she manage to complete her quest or be pulled in by the secrets of the manor?

A man haunted by his past...

Trapped within his own home and in the body of a hideous beast, Kris never wanted to share his prison with another. As much as Rose may draw him in with her beauty and stubborn strength, he knows she must escape before the next full moon. After all, he remembers all too well what happened to the previous caretaker.

The dead won't let him forget the blood on his hands.

*Available Now*

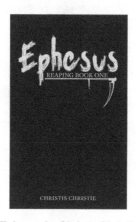

*Ephesus by Christis Christie*

**As a soul lost before it could live, Ephesus was gifted a special role—he must collect the dead.**

Ephesus has known no other existence than reaping souls, experiencing life only from the shadows. Remaining separate was easy, until the day he meets a unique little girl with an ability she should not possess.

But can friendships be nurtured when life and death aren't meant to mingle beyond the point of passing? Ephesus must navigate the world fulfilling his purpose while also balancing his newfound curiosity of the girl's life. However, when a threat arises, will it mean their ruin?

*Available Now*

**The Prince and the Puppet Thief by Justin Arnold**

**Welcome to the kingdom where princes kiss thieves, princesses dance with their handmaids at midnight, and non-binary magicians see to it that everyone gets their happy-ever-after.**

17-year-old Simon The Squirm has spent his life on the run- and he hates it. Breaking the law gives him anxiety, and he always forgets to carry a weapon. Being the son of the 2nd most feared villain in the kingdom has never been easy, but when an ill-conceived plan to steal the Lost Princess's slippers lands him in the dungeon, he makes up his mind to take the first opportunity at freedom.

Prince Marco isn't convinced he's the one to rescue the

lost Princess Isobel. Sure, he's a handsome and brave royal straight out of a fairy tale- but that doesn't mean he's ready to fall for the first damsel in distress who sends out an S.O.S. When he finds himself smitten with the sarcastic (if bumbling) Simon, a scheme is hatched to save both of them from a not-so-happily-ever-after.

The mission is simple: Simon must go in Marco's place to rescue the princess and defeat the wicked magician who stole her. But when it becomes clear that Princess Isobel would rather be saved by her handmaid, Prince Marco and Simon might just end up rescuing each other instead.

Perfect for fans of *The Two Princes* podcast and Sonan Chainani, *The Prince And The Puppet Thief* is a hilarious and swoon-worthy fairy tale rom-com by and for the LGBT community.

*Available Now*

*The P.A.N. by Jenny Hickman*

Since her parents were killed, Vivienne has always felt ungrounded, shuffled through the foster care system. Just when liberation finally seems possible — days before her eighteenth birthday — Vivienne is hospitalized with symptoms no one can explain.

The doctors may be puzzled, but Deacon, her mysterious new friend, claims she has an active Nevergene. His far-fetched diagnosis comes with a warning: she is about to become an involuntary test subject for Humanitarian Organization for Order and Knowledge — or HOOK. Vivienne can either escape to Neverland's Kensington

Academy and learn to fly (Did he really just say fly?) or risk sticking around to become a human lab rat. But accepting a place among The PAN means Vivienne must abandon her life and foster family to safeguard their secrets and hide in Neverland's shadows... forever.

*Available Now*

# Credits